BRETON ADVENTURE

by

JANE SHAW

THE CHILDREN'S PRESS
LONDON AND GLASGOW

CONTENTS

CHAPTER I

THEY ARRIVE

"D'YOU think you'll be all right?" Vanessa, standing with one hand on the carriage door of the train that was to take her to Paris and her husband, regarded her young sister and cousin doubtfully. "I wish I didn't have to dash off and meet John. But it isn't far from here to Madame's, and the one we've chosen seems the most fatherly of those villainous-looking taxi-drivers." She nodded towards the fatherly villain who would have been astounded at the character he was being given, but who, withdrawn a little from this scene of parting, was indeed watching them benevolently, a wide smile on his face. It was not every day that his little taxi, good little taxi as she was, struck such a fine bargain as to convey two English *mesdemoiselles* from here in St. Brieuc to a house near some obscure village called St. Brioc—a profitable journey. "And Caroline," Vanessa went on, "don't pay him a penny more than we agreed on. And Sara, dear, do wear your glasses, as Auntie said, and be careful you——"

("Marriage," thought Caroline gloomily, half-listening to her sister, "has done this girl no good. Like an old hen, clucking away; and she used to be quite decent.") "Yes," she said aloud. "Yes, yes, yes—I mean, no—of course he won't murder us on the road. You'd better hop in now, or the train will go, and you'll delay *darling* Johnnie a whole day—think how dreadful that would be: he would miss his conference or whatever he's after in Zurich. Where's that ass Sara? Hope your old car behaves, and you don't get stuck. What's that old boy doing with the tin trumpet? I'd have thought he was beyond that sort of thing. Oh, the guard, is he? Very queer, the French. He's going to give us a tune now from the look of him. Don't fuss, Vanessa; of course we'll be all right. I should get in, if I were you. Where's Sara?"

Vanessa negotiated the high step and slammed her carriage door, still muttering dark prophecies of disaster. The trumpet sounded, the train was slowly, reluctantly starting to pull out when confused shouts and sounds of a frantic scuffle came from somewhere in its inside. Vanessa disappeared, the door was hurled open, and a small figure catapulted out of the train, and, not being ready for the great height, landed rather ungracefully on all fours beside Caroline. As the train gathered speed Vanessa managed to shut the door and looked back at them with a face more anxious than ever, while the wind mercifully scattered the no doubt excellent advice she was making a last valiant effort to shout at the two girls.

"Gosh! That was a near thing, wasn't it, Caro? Well, I wasn't doing a thing—I was only having a look at the train, for I was getting a bit fed-up with old Van gassing away. Gosh, isn't it fun? Now we're absolutely alone in France: we might start by exploring St. Brieuc——"

"There's a taxi waiting, fat-head. And Madame waiting at the other end. Probably in a fever, trying to decipher all Vanessa's telegrams."

"Yes, all right. But look over there, that fruit stall—I'll just nip over and get some cherries." Caroline got herself into the taxi beside their luggage, and then turned round to see Sara staggering back under an enormous bag—it looked about half-a-stone—of cherries.

"Yes, it does seem rather a lot," she admitted, "but I kind of got mixed up with the French weights, and after I'd asked for two kilos instead of half a one I didn't like to let on I'd made a mistake. And anyway, I'm rather fond of cherries and we'll be jolly hungry before we get there and it's ages since we had lunch."

"It's exactly half an hour, and the house is about eight miles away—but never mind, let's see some cherries."

The fatherly villain shot away from the station with much strident blowing of horn, through the town and out into the country almost before the two had collected themselves.

"Hey, don't you think we ought to tell him he's driving on the wrong side?" said Sara, as, putting on her glasses, lest she should miss anything, she looked about her and wakened up to what was happening. "We'll hit something!"

"They always drive on the wrong side in France." Caroline spoke in the voice of one whom nothing could surprise. Sara was amazed, but did not waste much time thinking on the oddity of the French when so much more pleasure was to be derived from speculation as to Madame de St. Brioc and her house, Petit Chose—*à St. Brioc, Côtes-du-Nord*—which was to be their home for the next two months.

"I wonder if she'll be decent?" she mused aloud, getting to work on the cherries, and interrupting herself constantly to point out to Caroline a calvary by the road-side or the remarkable absence of noteworthy scenery—nothing but hillocks and low trees—or once, with great excitement, some peasant women in snowy caps doing their washing by a rather muddy-looking pool; Caroline, who somehow saw most things long before Sara, only grunting in reply. "After all, it's ages since your mother knew her at school in Switzerland—she may have gone all funny, like Vanessa, with being married and having a husband. And an eighteen-year-old son. He'll be frightful, of course—black as ink and very—very dapper. I wonder what the château will be like? Great stone place, I expect, wee slits for windows, suits of armour all over the place, and ghosts with clanking chains round every corner. Why didn't Auntie tell us more about it, now I come to think of it?"

"How could she? She's never seen it," Caroline answered. "She stayed with this Madame person in Paris once or twice, if that's what you're thinking of."

Sara was not thinking of anything very consecutively. The joy and thrill of the situation came over her again, and she cried, bouncing up and down a little, "Gosh, Caroline, isn't it marvellous? We'll have the most gorgeous adventures at last! Why don't you get more *excited*? Don't you wonder——"

"One looney's enough in this party, I should think." Caroline maintained her calm. "And what's the good of wondering? I know the house is on the cliffs above the sea and that there's a tennis-court—we'll see the rest for our-

selves in about half an hour, so keep cool. Are
you going to eat all the cherries?"

"Caroline!" Sara was off at a tangent. "What's
he slowing down for? Gosh, maybe he is going
to rob and murder us, after all. Oh, gosh!"

"Don't be idiotic. Although how Vanessa
could ever think he looked fatherly! Probably,
in spite of his face he's a perfectly nice man. And
he'll never suspect our money-bags, anyway."
Caroline grinned at the thought and Sara giggled.
"Maybe they were a good idea after all! But I
wouldn't tell Mummy that for the world."

These same bags had been a sore point. As
soon as their male parents, who were brothers, had
decided that any more such reports as came in
from school about Sara and Caroline's French
were not to be tolerated, and that, too, it was high
time they saw something of the world—"Why,
at their age you and I had been half over Europe
and could speak French, German, *and* Italian
fluently," Robert Storm had said rather boast-
fully, and rather inaccurately, to his brother, who
agreed—as soon then, as it was decided to send
the two off to stay with an old school friend of
Caroline's mother, their mothers had dashed off
and bought the offending bags.

"See, darlings," said Caroline's mother, as they
were gathered in her house, making plans, "you

buckle it round your waist, under your dress, and your money is absolutely safe. I wouldn't travel without one."

Sara and Caroline were affronted—"Go about with this thing on, and sticking out in a great lump? And when we want tuppence to buy a bar of chocolate do we undress?"

"I don't think it's at all likely you'll have enough money to make a lump," Mrs. Storm assured them. "And you haven't got the idea at all. You have ready money in your bags, and the rest, quite safely, in here. Invaluable things. Here you are, one each." The girls, as they might have known they would in the end, accepted the offending eccentricities meekly enough, certainly never thinking the time might come when they would actually be glad of them.

The car lurched to a stand-still and the villain, looking, to Sara's eyes, more and more unlike any respectable father she had ever seen, climbed down and came round and opened the door at Caroline's side. Sara's fingers dug deeply into Caroline's arm, which was no great help to her, trying as she was to put on her haughtiest expression and wondering if she could possibly manage to adopt a commanding and awe-inspiring tone in the French language. The villain, with a sinister smile, let fly a great volley of French,

accompanied by much pointing to the back of the
car and waving of arms.

"What's he saying?" said Sara, in an anxious
small voice, her faculties apparently paralyzed
with terror.

"Wants us to get out——"

"Wild horses," Sara announced, "won't drag
me from this car. I know what it is, Caro, it's a
hold-up. He's going to rob us and then abandon
us and beat off with our luggage and money and
everything. Where are you *going*? Caroline, don't
move!"

Caroline, to whom the villain had repeated
himself, even more vehemently but smiling
brightly the while, when Sara was indulging in
one of her imaginative flights, got out and
laughed round at her from the road.

"Come on, daftie, it's only a puncture. And
you're sitting on the tools." Sara bundled out,
very much relieved, and giggling a little.

"Honestly, Caroline, I thought my last hour
had come. *What* an escape! D'you think he'd
like me to help?"

"Not knowing you, he might. But you'd only
get dirty and probably wreck something vital."

The wheel was soon changed, in spite of Sara's
constant interruptions with offers of advice and
cherries: and the journey was resumed in the

friendliest of atmospheres. The villain, now positively benign, pushed open the glass slide separating them and flung conversation at them over his right shoulder—to Sara's alarm, for keeping his eye on the road didn't seem to strike him as at all part of his duties.

"Kerdic!" he shouted suddenly, as the taxi careered madly through a little village, scattering chickens. "The house, perhaps, is not far?" Caroline told him it lay somewhere between this village and St. Brioc, Sara having lapsed into a moody silence at the sight of Kerdic, an unprepossessing enough place certainly, with a dull, untidy, poverty-stricken air about it. He stopped then, rather abruptly—which did not improve either Sara's temper or the remains of the cherries which shot off her lap all over the floor—to ask after the whereabouts of Petit Chose.

"To the right," said a dismal peasant, waving vaguely at a landscape quite devoid of houses. Since there was nothing else to do, the villain drove straight on and in a little while, sure enough, turned off the main road into a narrow lane, overshadowed by trees, and inches deep in dust which rose in clouds behind them. They passed on the right a high house, painted pink, with grey shutters.

"Expect that's it," gloomed Sara, who hated

pink and who was suffering from reaction, suddenly very nervous and tired, what with the travelling and the excitement, the heat, and Vanessa's getting that telegram from John and deserting them. Madame was probably a monster, too—all this going to live with a strange family in a strange land, what a rotten idea it was anyway! "And where's the sea?" she wailed aloud. Caroline, well used to Sara's ups and downs, glanced at her quickly.

"Bear up," she advised. "We'll be there in a minute, I should think. And let's hope Madame has a spot of English, for I've had about as much French since we got to St. Malo this morning as I can be doing with. If the old villain would take his time and ask first he wouldn't have to do all this backing and turning and we wouldn't be choked with dust."

The villain, after an interchange of courtesies with a small girl who seemed set on driving her cows straight into the bonnet of the car, backed once more alongside a high wall they had already passed about three times until they came to a rather lovely pair of wrought-iron gates. The villain opened them with a flourish, drove in, and they were there.

The house, which they approached from the side, and which was no distance from the gate, was high, with pointed eaves, dazzling white in the sunlight, the windows flanked with green shutters. They got a quick impression of a rough lawn, flower beds and trees, masses of trees—but no sea was to be seen, not so much as a piece of seaweed or a small dancing wave.

"Oh, dear!" said Sara. "The house looks quite bright—but it's no château. Where are the cliffs? Where's the sea? And oh, gosh! *There's* Madame!"

On the doorstep a young woman had appeared; she was small and dark-skinned with curly hair like jet, and, on that hot summer's day, she was dressed completely in black. Except for her feet, which were encased, rather surprisingly, in white sand-shoes. As they climbed down and the villain handed out their luggage, she bobbed a curtsey and gabbled at them. Sara was quite beyond understanding any more French; Caroline, looking rather puzzled, turned to her cousin, drooping by her side.

"She's not Madame, anyway. Goodness knows where she is. Somebody or other has gone with the carriage to meet us at the station, for dear, clever Vanessa seemingly never mentioned we were coming by car. Better pay off the villain and get in." Sara showed a great inclination to cleave to the villain, their only friend amid this strangeness, but Caroline gave him his money and he departed, still smiling and saying, with proud command of languages and some suddenly awakened memory of an American tourist, "Okay, okay, good-bye!" They followed the little black person inside, into what seemed pitch darkness after the glare of the sun.

"Gosh, isn't it funereal?" whispered Sara, stumbling up a flight of wide, wooden stairs. The gloom seemed if anything to increase as they mounted; at the top of the stairs the white sand-shoes turned left, padded along a corridor, and their owner ushered the two girls into a big room, dim and crowded with heavy, elaborate furniture, the walls hung with dark, religious pictures, but having two little beds covered with the gayest patchwork counterpanes imaginable.

"That's the most cheerful thing I've seen in the last couple of hours," said Sara, flopping on one. Their guide, with a murmur of "hot water" disappeared and the girls could gaze round.

"*I* know why it's so dim," said Caroline briskly. "The shutters are all closed." She strode to one window, pushed the shutters back and looked out to the garden at the front, then to the window in the opposite wall, to the left of the door, and was equally hearty with that one. She leaned out.

"This is the back, I suppose. Help! What's

this? Sara!" she giggled? "I've found the tennis-
court!"

Sara joined her at the window, and looked on to
a space among the trees, roughly the shape of a
tennis-court, but with no netting, and deep in
gravel and leaves.

"Where?" she said, rather crossly. "You don't
mean that thing?"

"Of course! The French are so odd. Do they
play on it as it is, I wonder?"

The black one came back with two tall steam-
ing cans, returned a minute later with an even
larger pitcher of cold water, smiled on them and
departed. Sara started to wash, rather half-
heartedly, and their suitcases were brought in,
this time by an ancient man, obviously the
gardener from the mother-earth still clinging to
his sabots, who talked away, but seemingly without expecting an answer. Caroline was debating
with herself what oddity would appear next,
when a rumbling of wheels outside took her to
the front window and she leaned over as far as
she could without falling out altogether. She
cried:

"Lumme! Is *this* Madame?"

Sara hurried over, rubbing her face with a
towel, and then hurried back for her glasses
without which she couldn't see a thing at such a

distance; but by that time Madame, if *it* were Madame, had disappeared into the house.

"What *is* it?" Sara wanted to know.

"Wait!" Caroline cackled weakly. "You'll see!" so that Sara was quite unprepared for the enormously fat woman of middle age, clad also in deepest black and sand-shoes and crowned with a venerable bonnet, who knocked and entered. But she too dropped a curtsey, talking volubly, and handed over a letter. So at last, from the thin, spidery writing, they learned that Madame was desolated, but she had been urgently called away, to visit the sick, and that Marie la Cuisinière and Louise and Yvonne the maids would see to their comfort until her return, in time for dinner, she devoutly hoped. Marie la Cuisinière beamed at them, and told them she had awaited train after train, frantic with worry, but here they were, safe and sound, and so much the better. Then she took herself off, with promises of something to eat. That should have cheered Sara, who had collapsed on the bed again, but she was tired, suddenly desperately home-sick, and full of foreboding that this first visit abroad was going to be a dismal failure after all.

"What are you doing?" she asked Caroline truculently as she saw her fumbling with keys and the lock of her big case.

"Unpacking." Caroline's habitual placidity was unruffled.

"Well, you needn't, because I'm not staying. Nothing would induce me to stop a night in this dreadful house, with all those mad people screaming away in that ridiculous language. And they're all in mourning, too. I expect they murder strangers and bury them under the tennis-court, if it is a tennis-court. And then go into mourning for them. It's no use grinning like an ape. I *won't stay*."

"How d'you propose to get back to St. Malo?"

"I'll walk—every step of the road if I have to. I imagined an enormous great castle, right on the cliffs with the sea booming at the foot of them, and Madame with beautiful white hair and long, thin hands waiting to greet us. And a real tennis-court (not that I mind about that) and lovely gardens and maybe a peacock——" Caroline guffawed.

"You *are* a wee funny, Sara. Only you would have thought of a peacock. And Madame's not as old as Mummy, and she never mentioned a castle in her letters—matter of fact, I don't believe they're too well off."

"No, I dare say not, but I thought *all* the French lived in châteaux and her husband is a *marquis* after all, if she's Madame la Marquise de St. Brioc."

"Yes, but fathead, nobody in France bothers much about titles nowadays—they're two a penny. Madame never uses hers; Mummy only told you that bit because you're such a snob and she thought it might impress you."

"Well, I've been deceived, and I'm going home."

"All right," Caroline knew her Sara. "We'll go to-morrow, but we can't dash off without even seeing Madame, it would be frightfully rude and you wouldn't like that. If you're semi-clean we might wander downstairs and see about that food. I'm peckish. Here, comb your hair—it's like a mop. And put your specs on: you'll want to see the house before we go."

Downstairs, they found the smaller mourner for murdered strangers, who told them she was Yvonne, waiting for them in the hall, which they now saw to be a pleasant lounge, dim and cool, with a table and chairs scattered about. She led them through a glass door, under the staircase, into the *salle à manger*. Caroline was immensely taken with its cream walls, and floor of dark-red tiles, its long narrow refectory table, the old sideboard and the rush-bottomed chairs. French windows opened on a small gravel square, another part of the house forming one side, the maligned tennis-court another, and the garden the fourth.

Caroline poked Sara in the ribs. "Cheer up,"

she said. "Look, ancestors on the walls—very classy." So there were, three or four, not very old, but Sara, for all her romantic notions, was now herself again and more interested in what lay on the table: coffee and long roll-shaped things but soft—like cookies, Sara thought, and which she came later to know as *brioches*—very salt butter and very sweet jam. . . .

Feeling enormously better, they wandered into the garden, noticed the great profusion of roses and little else; and saw, with quickened interest, an old ruin through the trees. On the other side of the house lay a kitchen garden, where they smiled vaguely at the gardener, returned to his rightful labours, but didn't risk any conversation. Beyond were farm-buildings, and they could see a dusty path meandering off to the left. In front of the house, beyond the drive, was a low wall, and on the other side of it quite a little forest of tall fine trees. The high wall which shielded one side of the small property dwindled away by the trees.

"I feel grubby, rather, and as hot as anything in stockings and this tweed skirt," said Caroline, after their first quick tour of inspection. "Let's go back and get into something cooler. Why do mothers always think you'll be cold, travelling?"

"Just awkwardness," Sara undutifully affirmed.
"Just as they always make you take a mackintosh.
I hate my old school burberry, but Mummy
insisted, and I felt I'd better shut up or she'd think
of a brolly as well and that would have been the
last straw."

In their room they argued fiercely about the
relative merits of shorts or cotton dresses.

"What *possible* objection could Madame have to
shorts?" Sara wanted to know.

"If she's an old, white-haired specimen as you
think, she might have lots."

"Well, I'm going to wear mine anyway, later
on," said Sara.

"Of course; but you don't want to get her goat
the very first day. Better break her in gently."

It amused Caroline to notice that Sara, as she
talked, was pushing her clothes away into
drawers, but being quite a tactful young person
for her sixteen years she said nothing about this
change of plan, but went on with her own unpacking, quietly and competently. Sara, who
had no sooner got one drawer filled with under-
wear than she decided it was the only possible
place for her blouses and jumpers and hauled
everything out again on to the floor, was still in
the wildest confusion when Caroline had finished
and had retired to the top of her bed to watch.

"How on earth did you ever get packed?" she asked.

"Oh, Mummy did that! She had some idea it would be quicker."

Caroline laughed. "Yes, I seem to remember you sending telegram after telegram from school for more and more empty suitcases every time we were packing up for holidays."

"Gosh, packing at the end's easy if you've got plenty of cases," Sara said confidently. "You just fling everything in. It's packing to go to a place that gets me down. Where am I to put all this stuff? I've filled all the drawers you haven't bagged." Caroline took pity on her, and went to her rescue.

And there Madame found them, on the floor, giggling over a pair of the most disreputable old bedroom slippers to which Sara clung passionately and which she had slipped in when her mother wasn't looking. They sprang to their feet as she came in. They saw a short, slight figure wearing a white dust-coat over a linen skirt; she was bare-headed, dark-haired; her complexion was pale, she had soft brown eyes, a wide flexible mouth—and she did not look a day over thirty. She, in her turn, saw a strongly-contrasted couple with yet an odd resemblance: one was small and sturdy, her thick curls had reddish lights in them and were short enough to show oddly pointed ears which gave her a rather puck-like expression, accentuated by her vivid little face with its green eyes—under fly-away eyebrows—which she was screwing up shortsightedly to see the newcomer. The other was almost a head taller, as slim as a wand and very fair, her straight hair cut like a page-boy's; her wide grey eyes looked calmly and candidly forth on the world.

"Ah, my dear children!" Madame said, in French. "How very happy I am to see you!" Turning to the fair one she went on, in English, rather carefully and slowly. "Very surely, you are Caroline. You resemble so much your dear mother," and, to the girl's secret embarrassment, she kissed her warmly.

"We were beginning to think you didn't exist at all, after so many false alarms," Sara grinned at her, when she too had been kissed and welcomed. Madame, wringing her hands and casting up her eyes, exclaimed at the evil fortune which had called her away to see a sick friend, that day of all days.

"But tell me, why was it necessary for Vanessa to leave you?" she finished.

"Well, you see," Sara, delighted to find this young and friendly person instead of her white-haired Marquise and to hear English again, chattered like a magpie, "John has this conference in Zurich, he's a lecturer, you know, frightfully brainy and all that, and then they're going on to Vienna for him to take some course and having holidays at the same time before they collect us with Major Morris—that's the car, not a man— at the beginning of September. And he was taking the car over by Calais and then he wanted to be in Zurich a day sooner and Van gets into such a state when she's away from him, but it was a tremendous thrill seeing up on the board ' Telegram for Madame Douglas ' spelt all wrong too——"

Madame, hopelessly fogged, turned to Caroline for enlightenment.

"When we disembarked at St. Malo," Caroline said, slowly and clearly, shaking her head at Sara, "there was a telegram waiting for Vanessa, asking her to be in Paris to-day, instead of to-morrow——"

"That's just what I *said*," Sara interrupted eagerly.

"So," Caroline continued, disregarding her, "she took us to St. Brieuc and got us a taxi, and left for Paris at once. She said, would we say how sorry she was not to see you, and she will apologise herself when she comes in September. She was sure we were going to be murdered, getting here," she added.

"That, praise the saints, has not happened," Madame rejoiced. "Now I must wash myself. Descend to the *salon* when you are ready; dinner is at half-past seven—it is seven, nearly, now." And she wandered off.

"*Isn't* it all fun?" Sara was gloating again. "She looks awfully decent; and we're going to have real dinner, every night, instead of stupid old school supper. It's *much* more thrilling being by ourselves here instead of in Skye with the family, isn't it? Nothing exciting ever happens there, but we're bound to have adventures— unmask a gang of international crooks—" Sara's reading was entirely given over to thrillers —"or smugglers or something."

"Well, if we can find the sea, we might find some smugglers, though I'm sure I hope not— and meantime we'd better find the salon." Caroline, then and always, refused to pander to any nonsensical French pronunciation: she spoke the language with as little attempt at a French accent as possible, if she used a French word when speaking English she would pronounce it as nearly in the English fashion as she could. She found, as the days went on, that she could follow what was said without much difficulty; to speak it she was both too scornful and too lazy, but oddly enough, when she did make the effort, she was always understood. Sara, for her part, otherwise the despair of her French mistress, had an extraordinarily good accent of which she was rather proud. Rather than stay silent, she would have rushed into speech in Hindustani should the need have arisen; consequently she became much more fluent if more inaccurate than Caroline, but even so, as she did not always wait to discover what was being said to her, Caroline had often to go to her assistance and interpret.

But for this night only, as Madame said when they sat down to dinner, they would speak English, although from to-morrow she dared them to let her hear a word of it, for how furious their dear parents would be if they returned to Scotland with their French no better than when they came!

Dinner revealed more pitfalls for the unwary. They were waited on by Louise—the small, sharp-eyed, sharp-tongued maid Madame brought with her from Paris to Petit Chose every summer, the other servants being local—and whom they had not previously seen. They were in danger of starving that night through their inability to grasp the fact that when they said *merci*, whatever was being offered to them was whisked away. Caroline very soon realised that "please," not "thank you," was the magic word, but poor Sara, probably with some deep-rooted idea that *merci* was one word she really did know, never remembered and would have missed many a good thing if Louise or Madame and the rest of her family had not taken pity on her and made it into a little joke, asking patiently, "Do you mean 'thank-you, no,' or 'thank-you, yes'?"

And then the fork business! Shaken from her indulgent attitude towards the queerness of the French, Caroline's eyes were like two horrified saucers the first time she saw Madame wipe her knife and fork carefully on a piece of bread when she had finished a course, and lay them neatly by her plate. Sara, delighting in anything different, copied her; but Caroline was disgusted at such barbarity, and refusing to have any truck with it, left her knife and fork firmly on her plate. Louise, with a reproachful look, brought her clean ones. But no one got the better of Louise for long, for at lunch on the second day—and ever afterwards, when Caroline tried it on—seeing Caroline was making a habit of this, she held the plate out to her, saying firmly, "Your fork, Mademoiselle," until Caroline gave in and removed it.

Dinner itself was strange; the food was delicious, dripping with butter, but the two thought it peculiar that instead of meat, potatoes, and vegetables being served all together they became separate courses. "But it's a grand idea," Sara confided enthusiastically to Caroline, as they giggled over the day's events in their room that night, "because you can eat so much more of everything. I wonder if Mummy would adopt it? But I don't expect those awful boys" (which was the irreverent way Sara referred to her three brothers) "would ever stand for it."

After dinner Madame took them for a little promenade. They left the garden by a small gate in the left-hand wall and joined the path they had seen earlier. In two minutes they had left the wood on their right and were in more open country: another minute—and there was the sea, pale blue and misty in the evening light; and they were truly on the edge of the cliffs after all, and a narrow path twisted its way down to a little bay, far beneath them.

"That is where we bathe most often," Madame said, "although sometimes we go down to the village of St. Brioc. Look, down there—the village is hidden but you can just see the end of the quay and the lighthouse: it is sandy there, while our little *grève* is full of stones; but we have a *cabine*—what you call a—bathing-box?— no one else comes there, except the Duvals, a charming family who have a villa further along the cliffs over there." She waved a vague hand towards St. Brioc. "They, too, come every summer and you will meet them very soon— three girls, about your age, and a boy." The two, who felt they saw quite enough of girls about their own age at school, showed no marked enthusiasm, but they did agree with Madame that the *grève* was enchanting, and the panorama magnificent. They strenuously denied that they were tired after all that voyaging, or that they must now return to the house and go to bed.

"Doesn't it get quickly dark here?" Caroline said as they walked back. "At home or in Skye it's light nearly all night at the end of June."

Sara, who had been imagining that the darkness was due to her eyesight failing her rather more badly than usual, was considerably relieved to hear her, while Madame asked them endless questions about their home in the little village in the West of Scotland, and school, and their usual holiday places.

Once back at Petit Chose she lit their candles and despatched them firmly to bed. And the girls went quite meekly. Going to bed, for those two, by no means meant going to sleep, for although they were together always at school and often in the holidays their conversation never seemed to exhaust itself.

"I shall never," said Sara, washing, "as long as I live forget that awful arrival—like a nightmare, Madame after Madame turning up——"

"I did think Marie the Cook *was* Madame," Caroline giggled. "And actually I shouldn't have been surprised if the ancient gardener had suddenly torn off his false whiskers and announced he was Madame, having a little joke. You never can tell with the French."

"Gosh," was Sara's only, and rather irrelevant comment as she rolled into bed, "this is a gorgeous bed. There wasn't a decent chair in the *salon*, nothing but silly wee things with spindly legs, but the French do seem to know about beds. I'm not a bit sleepy, are you?"

"Not a bit," answered Caroline, burrowing into her pillows.

In two minutes they were both sound asleep.

CHAPTER II

THEY MEET ARTICHOKES, AJAX—AND RAYMOND

THE next thing Sara knew, it was morning, the warm sun was streaming in the open window by the head of her bed, and the queerest noise was going on underneath her. Half-awake, it took her some time to realise it was the quick rattle of French voices, a staccato murmur too distant to distinguish, coming from the kitchen below. Caroline, in the other little bed beyond the window, still lay like a log, and after an unsuccessful attempt to waken her by means of two badly-aimed slippers, Sara amused herself by trying to count the different colours in her patchwork cover, and wondering how long it would be till breakfast-time and what there would be to eat and whether some one would call them or if they were supposed to know by instinct or something when to get up.

Then there was a knock on the door and Yvonne, smiling and saying good-day, came in bearing a huge tray which she laid on the little table at the window between the two beds, which they could both reach without getting up.

"Fun!" thought Sara. "Breakfast in bed! How nice of Madame," she thought, not realizing that the entire Petit Chose household breakfasted in their rooms every day and only appeared downstairs at the civilised hour of ten o'clock or so. "Hey, Caroline," she shouted at the pitch of her not inadequate lungs, "wake up! Breakfast!"

"Go away and leave me alone," Caroline grunted. "Don't want any breakfast."

"What a lazy toad you are," said Sara, with the dreadful briskness of those who are bright in the mornings. "Do wake up, it's right here at your nose, and you've only to stretch out a hand. And just *feel* the lovely sun!"

Caroline looked at her over the edge of the sheet with one cold eye, hunched the bed-clothes closer round her and turned over without speaking. But it was no use, Sara had murdered sleep, so she reluctantly hauled herself upright against her pillows and rescued, just in time, her share of the food.

If at home any one had offered either of them such a breakfast as they ate at Petit Chose every morning there would have been an uproar— stacks of thickly-cut bread which seemed to have more holes in it than anything else, the salt butter in little crocks, and huge cups, like young basins, of coffee.

"What's this stuff, anyway?" Caroline queried

sourly, holding a slice of bread up to the light. "Crust and holes, that's all it is, like a sieve. I could do with a good plate of bacon and eggs. And I hate breakfast in bed, anyway."

"You're a cross, ungrateful wretch," Sara told her smugly, for however Caroline might deplore her lost bacon and eggs, Sara revelled in *petit déjeuner*. That did not of course stop her having her great idea for brighter breakfasts—but that was later.

Caroline seemed to have the glooms properly this morning.

"Do you realise that there's no bathroom in this house?" she asked.

"Well, there's the sea—and Madame looks clean enough. By the way, Caro, where *are* the rest of the family? Armand and Raymond she kept talking about last night?"

"They arrive in a day or two, apparently— with Ajax, whoever he may be: Armand is her spouse and Raymond is the son."

"Oh! I shudder to think what he'll be like. D'you remember that French boy who came to Skye with the Stuarts one summer, or weren't you there? Well, he was as fat as a barrel and had long, long, hair, and he wore a bow tie and a tweed suit, the kind of tweed a girl would wear, and the coat was all pleats and tucks and leather buttons. He was terribly proud of it, too—told me it was an English 'sporting'; but the first time Mummy saw him she called him 'Mademoiselle' and he was simply livid. He was an awful creature—didn't play any games, kept complaining about *courants d'air*, and wouldn't bathe because the water was so cold. Raymond will be just like that."

"Well, I don't blame him for not bathing in that sea; and the French don't think such a lot of games as we do, I believe, although he sounds rather wet, I must say. I'd rather Raymond was more decent than that, but he probably won't bother with us anyway, seeing he's eighteen."

"Or we won't bother with him." Raymond was dismissed, and Sara, bursting with energy, hustled Caroline out of bed and down to the *salon*, much too early for her liking. It was a pleasant room, light and sunny, with faded rose-pink curtains, rather littered with little tables and the frail gilt chairs Sara so much despised, but having large French windows in three walls from which two stone steps led to the gardens or the square by the dining-room; a piano stood in one corner and a writing-desk in another.

"Nice," said Sara, poking about. "But I do think it's odd to find that French houses really have French windows, don't you?"

Caroline thought it was the most natural thing in the world, but hadn't time to say so before Madame came in and bade them good-morning, with anxious enquiries as to the comfort of the night. "The tide is out this morning, so we can't bathe," she went on, "but would it amuse you to come down to St. Brioc with me, while I do some shopping? I always go in the *voiture* if the car is not here, but poor Pipi is lame to-day, so"—with a deep sigh—"we shall have to go on foot. Can you bear it, do you think?"

Sara assured her, to her surprise, that they often went for walks deliberately at home, wondering at the same time what funny sort of a place this was where bathing was only possible at high tide. (One afternoon some time later, Sara, who liked to prove things for herself, declared that they ought to put this to the test: Caroline thought it was probably a waste of time, but wanted a bathe anyway, so they put on their bathing dresses at the *grève*, although the sea was not actually in sight. They walked hopefully over wet sand for what seemed about a mile, and less hopefully over sand and sea-weed for another: they did finally reach the sea, all right, but as it obstinately refused to become any deeper than knee-high, they gave up in disgust, before they reached home and mother, Caroline said. And Sara thereafter was more ready to believe that when Madame said there was no bathing, there *was* no bathing.)

As they left the house Caroline relieved Madame of a huge string bag, hoping it wasn't going to be quite filled before they got back. The two girls had slung over their shoulders their little leather bags from which, on holiday and in the country, they were never parted and which they used for every purpose except that for which they were designed, namely carrying golf-balls. Madame admired them, but was amazed that at home they played golf and enjoyed great long walks and such strenuous things.

They went down to St. Brioc by a short-cut, a narrow cliff path on one side lined with high hedges thick with honeysuckle whose name of *chèvrefeuille* they liked. They came on some goats presently a little lower down, clanking their chains at the end of long tethers and nosing up to them inquisitively. At the foot of the path they passed some villas, half hidden by waving tamarisks, and the one little hotel. Beyond them the bay opened out to their right, children playing on the sands, and some fishing-boats, their red sails furled, high and dry in the shelter of the long quay with the lighthouse standing at its very end. On the left lay more villas, their little gardens massed with hydrangeas not yet in bloom, but faintly green. Facing the bay, along the quay, stretched a smooth curve of high, stone houses, broken at last by the *Hôtel de Ville* which bore notices and placards of forthcoming diversions for the villagers. Crossing the quay, Madame led them through a narrow cleft between high rocks to see another little bay encircled by towering cliffs.

Then they turned to the serious business of shopping. On Madame's advice they bought themselves *espadrilles* like her own, thin linen beach shoes with rope soles. They visited the butcher and the grocer and the baker, who were all delighted to see Madame, paying them her first visit for the summer, and asked solicitously for Monsieur and affectionately for M. Raymond. Then Madame thought the girls might like a cake (although she warned them that St. Brioc had only a little village shop, not a real *pâtisserie* like St. Brieuc or St. Quay) and they went right into the shop-window armed with a plate and picked up what they wanted, which Caroline considered very queer and bad for Sara, who would have liked to sample everything. Such luscious cakes they were, too. "And the funny bit is," said Sara, "they look so unexciting. Whereas our cakes look really very pretty, and yet inside there's usually nothing but mouldy old sponge-

cake." Then Madame sent them off to explore on
their own for a little, while she paid another
call.

Sara adored shops and they poked into as many
as they could find, buying stamps and postcards
and chocolate. They discovered one lovely one
full of carved wood and toys and bric-a-brac, but
regretfully left it till they had more time. They
did go into one little place, full of lace and wool
and pieces of embroidery, since Sara, who was
subject to sudden enthusiasms, decided she simply
must have something to sew. The woman in the
shop was young and friendly and full of conversation, and brought forth half her stock while Sara
dithered, favouring now a cushion with dragon-
flies on it, now a table-centre, with poppies, and
finished by taking both. Even Caroline, who, as
any mistress at school would have testified, could
do nothing more successfully and for a longer
period than most people, was inspired by all this
promise of industry to buy some pink wool and
great fat knitting pins, to knit a bed jacket some
one had told her was "awfully quick and absolutely foolproof."

And there they might have been yet, choosing
bright silks for Sara, if Madame had not found
them and hurried them home to lunch.

In the afternoon they found the little rocky

grève delightful for bathing, in spite of the pebbles, and the water warmer than they had dreamed possible.

"Like a hot bath," Caroline exulted, "and hotter than most of the ones I get at school," and they spent the afternoon very pleasantly in and out of the sea, and sunbathing on flat rocks that became almost too hot to touch. As the day passed Sara realised, now Madame was insisting on French, that her knowledge of that language, thrust upon her with so much mutual suffering by poor little Mademoiselle at school, was definitely inadequate, so she attacked it with spirit, and more or less success. Caroline scarcely opened her mouth unless directly addressed, although when she heard Madame tell Sara that she must try to *think* in French she roused herself to hoot derisively and volunteer the information that it wasn't possible, because Sara didn't even think in English.

They did some more reconnoitring on the way home, Madame showing them the *vieux jardin* which, surrounded by a high wall, lay among the trees in front of the house. It was huge, and neglected; there was an old shed which apparently housed Raymond's canoe during the winter, and some healthy-looking gooseberry bushes which made Sara think that a visit to that warm, peaceful spot one day with their sewing would be a good idea. . . .

"Now what's coming?" thought Sara, at dinner, watching Caroline's expression of faint surprise. It annoyed Sara rather that from where Caroline sat she could see what queer dish was being carried in next without seeming too eager for her food, but she consoled herself with the reflection that as she had left her specs upstairs she couldn't have seen anyway. The dish of dark-green footballs thrust at her by Louise came therefore as a complete shock. But she helped herself to one and set about it with a will. Caroline waited for a lead, as to the method of attack; she dare not catch Sara's eye, but stripped and sucked her artichokes as if they had been her staple diet for years, wondering what Sara was finding to chew so valiantly and with such a face of anguish.

When dinner was over, "Out of here, quick!" Sara muttered, and announced to Madame that they were anxious for another little promenade. Almost before her surprised but resigned permission was spoken they were over the low wall at the foot of the garden, through the wood, skirting the *vieux jardin* and out on the open spaces above the cliffs.

Caroline went into one of her fits of silent

laughter as Sara shamefacedly opened her hand-kerchief and turned out some mangled green masses.

"Artichokes, were they? What kind of food is that for growing girls? I was so ravenous I didn't watch Madame, but after I'd got three revolting lumps into my napkin I thought there must be another method of coping with the horrors. How was I to know they weren't for eating, only for sucking? And of *course* I couldn't get rid of them." Sara was laughing too now, and Caroline wiped her eyes; but whenever they looked at the deceased artichoke and thought of what Sara had gone through in her efforts to hide her ignorance they went into another fit of giggles, until they were rolling on the grass, much to the amaze-ment of an old peasant who dropped his mouth open and gaped at them as he passed. That set them off again, until their tummies were so sore they simply had to stop. They finally staggered to their feet and wandered weakly to the edge of the cliff without paying much attention to where they were going.

"I say, look!" said Caroline, still giggling spasmodically: "there's another little bay down there, and what might almost be a very faint path——"

"I can't see any path," said Sara, peering, "but

we might explore. Maybe it's a haunt of smugglers."

"You and your smugglers! We'll explore it, all the same—but it's too late to-night; it'll soon be getting dark, and Madame will be sending Louise after us."

"We'll come to-morrow if we can get away from the invasion. Did *you* manage to grasp from Madame at dinner who exactly is arriving to-morrow?"

"Only three, as far as I could make out," said Caroline. "Monsieur himself, who's a bit absent-minded and you have to bawl at him if you want him to pay any attention; Raymond, and some person called Ajax."

"Oh, yes, I wondered who he was: Madame said he was *adorable*. Friend of Raymond's maybe—he sounds frightful, if he's *adorable*, but we'll know the worst to-morrow."

The worst was nothing like what they expected. They were lying by themselves sun-bathing at the *grève* the next afternoon, when a young man, slight, but with a body which seemed to be entirely composed of springs, came bounding down the path with a dog at his heels. Coming over to the girls, he grinned till his eyes crinkled up and disappeared, shook hands, and announced himself as Raymond. Rather dazed, they inspected him. To begin with, he was fair (which was in itself a shock to Sara, who fondly imagined all Frenchmen to be dark) and lean, with clear-cut features and rather hollow cheeks; his hazel eyes laughed and his wide mouth laughed, and his tongue did not rest for a second. His clothes were in no way exceptional, for he was wearing a perfectly normal pair of shorts, a white shirt and *espadrilles*. Just let loose from the city, he was obviously bursting with energy and high spirits.

"Wait," he said, "only one very little minute and I will bathe with you," and he leapt away to change, the dog barking round him.

Caroline cocked an eyebrow at Sara. "You're a good prophet, I must say. He's not wearing a ' sporting,' and he looks sporting enough to run you off your feet. And another thing, I bet you anything that that"—pointing to the dog which lay panting outside the *cabine*—"is Ajax."

She was right. When Raymond came forth he introduced them to the white poodle which, though rather comic, was a fine-looking fellow.

"Ah, yes, he is handsome," Raymond agreed, "but he has no brains, this poor Ajax."

They had a very jolly bathe, although Raymond promised them better fun when he had looked out his canoe. "We shall paint it to-morrow, and I will teach you how to paddle. And look, you must teach me English, for I do not speak it at all well, like Maman." He suddenly began splashing madly about. "Oh! How happy I am to be back here, after Paris."

They dressed and climbed slowly home, Raymond practising his English already. There was a startling change when he did so; his accent was very broken and rather fascinating, but he was so slow and hesitant that he was like another person, and he would very soon grin, give it up with a shrug, and gabble what he wanted to say in French. There was a lot of giggling, and all three managed to understand each other pretty well.

Monsieur was tall, with grizzled hair and moustache, and very charming to his young guests.

"Doesn't Raymond shout at his papa, though?" said Sara, in bed that night. "No one else does and he seems to pay attention all right. Gosh, French husbands and wives seem to be terribly devoted to each other, don't they?"

"Mm. A bit overdone for my taste," Caroline replied.

Sara giggled. "And I'd like to see the boys fussing round Mummy the way Raymond does. I wonder if I could get them to kiss my hand?"

"Not correct. You need to be a married woman."

"Oh? Well, maybe they wouldn't have, anyway. But I think it's rather nice myself—I like people to show their feelings a bit, too. Not like you, you old image, is it?"

Sara received no answer to her question. "It's a most maddening habit that of Caro's," she reflected, "going off to sleep bang in the middle of a conversation. Bright as a bee one minute and the next she's sound asleep. And I never know how long I've been talking to myself. I've a jolly good mind to waken her up and ask her, only she'd probably throw something at me. I'll tick her off about it to-morrow . . . to-morrow. . . ."

And Sara, too, slept.

CHAPTER III

SURGICAL INTERLUDE

"YOU will get a sunstroke, Sara, sitting there."

"Oh, *no*, Madame, thanks awfully all the same, honestly, I won't! I'm quite used to no hat and bare arms," Sara assured Madame from her favourite seat on the steps of the *salon* window. She was writing letters, and it was the hottest seat she could have chosen. Caroline was in the *salon*, doing nothing, looking cool and lazy.

"You will, you know, fathead," she put in. "French sun isn't like Scottish sun. Or at least you'll get horribly burnt."

"But I *want* a beautiful tan, like yours."

"Yes, but I dare say you won't get it," replied Caroline complacently. "You know you always go a boiled red before you get the least bit brown; but I just go brown straight away."

"Mm, you've got a tough hide," mumbled Sara. "' With - very - much - love - and - kisses - your - only - and - most - dutiful - daughter - Sara.' And that's *that* done. Come on. Let's go down to the *grève* now. Where's Raymond? Madame, are you coming? Come *on*, Caro! We're wasting a whole afternoon of lovely tide, in its proper place for once instead of half-way to Dover." And considering that Caroline had been waiting a good hour without a murmur while Sara did her duty by her parents, her lack of reply was commendable.

So they bathed, and sun-bathed and lounged in the garden again, and the next day even the optim- istic Sara was regarding her arms with some doubt. They were red and angry-looking and tender to a degree, and two enormous blisters, **as big as** the top of a tea-cup, flanked by smaller and less dramatic-looking ones, had risen above her elbows.

" Oh, gosh! They're a bit of a mess, aren't they, Caro? Isn't it a queer, and a very unfair thing, the way you're always right? What on earth shall I do with them, great lumps of raw meat?"

Madame was horrified, and exclaimed to heaven on the dangers of sitting in the sun, the folly of young girls in general and of the unfortunate Sara in particular. But her peroration finished on a more hopeful note, and with the magic word *Inotyol* on her lips she hurried away, to return with a yellow tube and breath for another dis- course, this time on the virtues of her remedy.

Sara unscrewed the cap and sniffed suspiciously.

" Smells nasty enough to cure anything," she muttered to Caroline in English. " Thanks awfully, Madame, I'll go and slap some on."

But Caroline stopped her. "Don't you ever listen? Night, angel-child, bed-time, Madame says: put it on thick and bind your arm up with bandages or strips of linen or something she's going to give you."

When bed-time came, more difficulties:

"You know, Sara," said Caroline reasonably, "I can't see what good this stuff will be when those great balloons of blisters are sitting there."

"No, that's true," Sara agreed. "Stick a pin in them," she suggested, with all the enthusiasm of a pioneer. "Oh, all right, a needle then! *Nothing* could be more hygienic. And we'll sterilize it, too, if you insist—no boiling water, of course, but there's the candle flame."

At the proceedings of the next ten minutes the blood of Sara's father, a surgeon of some repute, would have run cold. The needle dragged from Sara's embroidery was solemnly held in the candle flame. The fact that it immediately turned black upset Caroline considerably, but Sara soothed her by wiping it on her handkerchief, of all things, and the operation began. . . .

"And if you ask me, I was pretty brave," said Sara, when it was all over, the stiff yellow paste smelling strongly of antiseptic smoothed on, the arms bandaged, and the two rather exhausted girls safely in bed, the candle out.

"If you call screaming the house down whenever I and the needle came within five yards of
you, and moaning like a soul in torment when I
was putting on the doings, being brave, then you
were——" Caroline answered.

"Oh, blow!" Sara thought it was quite time
this line of conversation should cease; "I've
forgotten to do my teeth."

"Skip them for this once. Oh, all right, all right,
but light a candle for the love of goodness or
you'll fall out of the window or something!"

"Well, but I can't light the candle because I
dropped the matches behind the chest of drawers.
I'll be all right, it's not too dark. See, I'm manag-
ing—ow!—beautifully." She reached the wash-
hand-stand more or less unscathed.

"Honestly, Sara," Caroline's voice was sleepy
and affectionate, "people have been shut up in
looney-bins for doing once the things you do every
five minutes. If you ask me——" But Caroline's
great thought was doomed to be lost for ever,
for there broke in on it a cry of real distress,
followed by sundry chokings and splutterings.

Caroline sat up in bed, giggling helplessly.

"Don't mind how much nasty *Inotyol* you use,
little frog. We'll put tooth-paste on your poor
little arms to-morrow instead."

CHAPTER IV

SARA CATCHES A BURGLAR

LUNCH-TIME next day seemed to Sara a perfectly sensible time to regale Raymond with the more unsavoury details of the previous night's operations. She had had a lovely time in the morning telling the entire staff all about it, for they one and all entered whole-heartedly into every domestic happening small or large, and had inquired anxiously for poor Mademoiselle's *coup de soleil* and had suggested various infallible remedies culled from peasant grandmothers, while Madame, to Sara's horror, talked seriously of summoning a doctor. But Raymond had been off on his own, painting his boat, or some such ploy, so now he was the very willing audience; and with a grin on his face bawled the best bits at his father, sitting opposite.

"I'm not stone deaf, you know, Raymond," Monsieur put in patiently, having commented suitably on Sara's misfortune, and Sara laughed with him at Raymond's look of surprise, for she and Caroline had always much ado to control themselves over Raymond's usual mode of addressing his father as if he had to make himself heard from St. Brioc to Paris.

"Raymond," said Madame, "I had a telephone message from Michel this morning. He has been detained and will not arrive here to-night until it is late. So will you wait up for him and see his car safely into the shed and that he has something to eat." She turned to Caroline. "It is my cousin who is coming to stay for a few days, motoring from his house in Cannes, a most enchanting place. You will like him, I think, he is so gay, so lively—and a very special favourite of Raymond's." So Caroline, preferring the conversation of others to the sound of her own voice as was her custom, gleaned some information which Sara, at the noisy end of the table, missed entirely.

That afternoon the three young people were to go to have tea with the Duvals, whom the girls had met some days before. Mme. Duval herself, they decided, was rather a pet, but how she talked! Ever on, without a pause, fortunately, for any reply, and about three times as fast as any other of the French, although, goodness knows, *they* all seemed to talk fast enough. There was Régine, about Raymond's age, dark and rather handsome; then Monique, blonde and good-natured and quieter than the others; next came Miette, whose real name they never discovered, also of a good

size—"some crumb!" Sara had said rudely when
she found, to her intense delight, the meaning of
the unhappy child's nickname—but pretty, with
dark, dancing eyes; and Pierre, a big, overgrown
youth whose voice was cracking in a most alarm-
ing way, and who was also full of good nature.

"Only four of them!" Caroline would say in
surprise, discussing them with Sara and wondering why, for all their good-nature, they didn't
like them better: "they always seem more like a
dozen to me."

"Maybe it's the comic times they visit at that
annoys us," Sara suggested. For the Duvals had a
curious habit of paying a morning call just when
Louise had announced lunch. They would swarm
in, kiss Madame many times on each cheek (and
Sara always insisted that once she saw Miette kiss
her on the back of the neck when she couldn't get
in at the front). Then they would shake hands
with the rest of the company—"*Bonjour*, Sara!
Bonjour, Caroline!"—and Caroline could never
make up her mind whether Pierre's limp, damp
paw or Régine's pulverising grip annoyed her
more. Then they would chatter, while Sara
hopped crossly from foot to foot thinking of the
lovely soup getting colder and colder. Finally,
Madame would send them away—and the kissing
and hand-shaking performance had to be gone

through again. No matter how recently they had seen the girls, the Duvals one and all shook hands, until it became quite a game with them to see how often, without downright rudeness, it could be avoided. But the Duvals always won. Their final victory, after which the two gave up the struggle and shook hands with as good a grace as they could muster, was celebrated one morning a few weeks later at the *grève*. Caroline and Sara were in the water, duck-diving and trying to stand on their hands, with much shouting and spluttering, when the horde was sighted coming down the path.

"We've beaten them at last!" exulted Sara. "They'll never shake hands in the sea!" But Sara was wrong. Once into their bathing-dresses, they advanced grimly, wet hands extended, "*Bonjour*, Sara! *Bonjour*, Caroline!" And they never understood why Sara and Caroline were so full of giggles that morning.

Still, they admitted, it was very nice of the Duvals to ask them to *goûter*.

"It's a good name for it, too! A taste! But maybe, seeing we're visitors, they'll have something more than pale brown water and bread," said Sara, who was fond of her food.

"I'm afraid," sighed Caroline, "that tea is a meal the French just don't understand. You'd think, when they give us such luscious meals at other times they could make a bit more effort over tea. And Louise or Marie the cook coming smiling in—' You take *goûter*, to-day? '—as if it were something worth taking."

"It's the boiled milk with the skin on the top that I can't face," confided Sara, but Caroline felt that their French friends' habit of dipping bread, both buttered *and* with jam on it, into their tea was infinitely worse.

However, Mme. Duval did not fail them. Tea was in the garden, and much as usual, but enlivened with an excellent sponge-cake. Sara had to be severely hacked on the ankle under the table before she would show any decency.

And all the time Mme. Duval talked; which would have been all right if Sara hadn't decided that as the perfect guest she was in duty bound to give her a run for her money, and, in spite of the language difficulty, kept her end up nobly. The noise was terrific. As an under-tone to the duettists, Raymond was teasing Miette and Ajax indiscriminately, which Miette enjoyed and Ajax fairly hated, but hadn't enough independence of spirit to resent except by occasionally giving one of his penetrating barks; Régine and Monique, doing their best, were finding the monosyllabic Caroline rather heavy going. Pierre was talking to himself. When at length a rather stunned

Caroline heard Sara confiding that her little dog at home, Toots by name, was half terrier, half Spaniard, she thought it was time to take steps. So, with nods and winks, she enlisted Raymond, who was adored, and excessively bored by all the Duvals, and before long they had haled Sara off, still talking.

"The *things* you were saying to that poor lady! And I only heard about a quarter of them," said Caroline as the three walked up the dusty lane home to Petit Chose, the little scarlet poppies thick in the corn on either side and flaunting down the banks.

"Oh, gosh! Was my French awful?" Sara exclaimed in dismay and—certainly unjustifiable —surprise. "You know, Raymond, I'll say this for the French," she went on magnanimously, "you listen to our most ghastly howlers without batting an eye. It's very sweet and polite of you, but it doesn't help an earnest student of the language. Now, we help you, Raymond——"

"Yes, roar with laughter whenever he opens his mouth," said Caroline. But Raymond only grinned and said that he, being a particularly pleasant person, thrived on such treatment. . . .

Whether it was her sore arms, or Fate, mindful of her thirst for adventure, who kept jogging her awake, but that night Sara could not sleep. She dozed fitfully at first, but finally lay wide awake, sleep seemingly banished for ever. As she was normally an extremely good sleeper, she felt very badly treated.

"Gosh, what a night I'm having! . . . Lying awake here for hours and hours—Gosh, my arms are sore if I move! . . . There's a car—on the road somewhere—what on earth are they doing in this out-of-the-way spot? Lost, I expect. . . . Oh, dear, can I never get to sleep? . . . Lying here all alone, nobody else awake. . . . Don't suppose I should waken Caroline to talk to me. . . . Caro! Caro-o-o! . . . Oh, all right, you selfish beast, lie there and snore away! I might be lying here dying for all you care. . . . Dying of thirst. . . . Starving—starving! Why, of course! I'm ravenous, that's what's the matter, ravenous. People *never* can sleep when they're hungry. And we bought some Toblerone to-day. It's in a drawer somewhere, I brought it up—oh no, blow! Caroline said bring it up and I forgot. It's in the *salon*, on the bureau. Oh, dear, I *loathe* creeping about in the dark and I don't know where my specs are anyway. But I must have something to eat or I'll pass out. . . . Would they take my body back to Scotland, I wonder? Poor old John, if he and Vanessa have to cart a corpse home in Major Morris. . . . I'll jolly well go and get that chocolate—anything would be better than dying, and I'll be like a little mouse and not make a sound." She began badly by knocking over the candlestick. Caroline grunted and turned over. Fate might have given her a jolt, but Caroline slept on. Unsuccessful groping retrieved neither matches nor candle.

"I'll manage without," Sara decided as she struggled into her dressing-gown and slippers. She opened the door softly, not without a qualm, yet negotiated the length of corridor past Madame's door quite confidently, but the staircase was inky black, and fear stirred within her. All her store of lurid ghost stories, of dark deeds in old country houses leaped into her mind unbidden and certainly unwelcomed. Every stair, as she put a tentative foot on it, seemed to make a noise like the crack of a whip, and she paused on each one, shaking. All round her the old house groaned and trembled. Ghosts of dead de St. Briocs, sad spirits driven from their graves, forced to haunt the night for their sins, were stretching out fluttering hands to stop the intruder, brushing her with frail fingers, whispering, rustling.

"Oh, gosh, I wish I'd brought a candle! Oh, gosh, I wish I hadn't come!" The creak of the bottom step made her jump as if she had been shot; but now she had only to cross the hall, which seemed lighter, somehow, and she would be in the *salon*—of the return journey she dared not think. As she cautiously advanced, something made her turn her head to the right—and her heart stopped. There was a light in the *salle à manger*, shining dimly through the half-open door.

And then Sara was really brave. She moved, very slowly, very quietly, towards the dining-room. She did not know what ghastly feast she might witness, of chapfallen spectres with hollows where eyes should be, sitting round the grim board, holding in fleshless hands skulls instead of cups. But Sara had that kind of courage which, her imagination alive to every horror, her very soul filled with fear, made her go on. Or maybe it was just curiosity—but she went on. When she reached the doorway, her teeth clenched to stop their chattering, she could have cried with relief—even her short-sighted eyes could tell that that figure was human. He had his back to her, and as she watched he laid something, which glittered, in the light of a solitary candle, on the table and moved over to the sideboard.

"Well, of all the cheek!" thought Sara. "A burglar! . . . Gosh, what'll I do? The maids won't be any good, and by the time I creep upstairs again"—her blood froze at the very idea—

"and waken Raymond and Monsieur, he'll be off. If I yell, he'll biff me on the head and escape out the window. What'll I *do*? Pinching darling Madame's silver, the beast!" The short, blurred figure was indeed busily emptying the sideboard. "I'll have to go for him myself and then yell. Throw something over his head—a carpet? A rug?—*My dressing-gown*. Thank goodness Mummy made me bring my camel-hair one." She slipped her arms out, gathered it in front of her, made a quick silent dash across the red-tiled floor, had it over the man's head, twisted her leg round his, and brought him down with a crash before he suspected her existence.

"Help! Help!" she yelled. "Oh, bother it, that's no good—*Au secours! Au secours!* What an idiotic language this is. *Au feu! Au secours!*" She moved from her strategic position on the *voleur's* head to his chest, for his arms were violently trying to get free of the thick folds.

"Help! Help!" as she bounced up and down. "Caroline! Raymond!—Oh, gosh, there's a gang! I'm going to be murdered." For another figure had appeared at the open French window, muffled in a great-coat, a lantern held aloft showing his evil, grinning face.

"What in the name of heaven is happening?" Monsieur had come at last, Madame and Caroline crowding behind him, the maids a twittering chorus in the background. "Michel, you have arrived then! Where is Raymond? *What are you sitting on*, Mademoiselle?"

"I've a horrible feeling it's Raymond," said Sara. . . .

"If you could have seen your face! And bobbing up and down like a cork on the water," Caroline gasped, weak with laughing, when they were both safely back in bed again.

"Well, Raymond would keep heaving about. Gosh, I hope he's all right; he looked a bit queer when he got up, and I did bang his head on the floor once—oh, dear, I feel such an ass! And fed up, too, because I did think it was an adventure at last. I suppose I really ought to wear my specs, but it was dark and I couldn't find the beastly things, anyway. P'raps if I got those what d'you call 'ems on a chain——" Caroline had a vision of Sara with her small, elfin face, gazing solemnly on the world from behind a lorgnette, and spluttered again, but she stopped laughing when she heard Sara hop out of bed and start to fumble for her slippers.

"*Now*, what's the matter?" she demanded.

"I just remembered that I never got my chocolate—I'll run and get it."

"Over my dead body," said Caroline.

CHAPTER V

SARA JOINS THE NAVY

RAYMOND was not a jot the worse for having had his head thumped viciously on the floor, and his sense of humour fortunately proved equal to the strain: while as for Michel, he appointed himself the champion of a rather subdued Sara against the great flights of wit indulged in by Caroline and Raymond. Not to be outdone in politeness she assured him that, now she could see him properly, he really didn't look a bit like a gang, and anyway it was a jolly funny time to arrive at a person's house—and by the dining-room window, too, even if it was nearer the garage than the front door.

So they were soon the very best of friends, the fact that Michel spoke excellent English, although with rather a harsh, clipped accent, being a great point in his favour. Madame might frown as severely as she could, but whenever they were out of her sight, English they spoke; even Raymond made great strides, and Sara would crow with delight whenever Michel got his slang mixed, and assure him earnestly that people really didn't say "ripping" very much nowadays.

Sometimes Michel would desert them, go off with Monsieur or Madame somewhere; and always after dinner he would play bridge with them very solemnly, roping in Raymond for a fourth, or Mme. Duval perhaps would come over. Her brood came at her heels and the young people would be sent out of the way into the hall to play Vingt-et-un for shells which pleased nobody except Sara, who always won; or *Le Nain Jaune*, which invariably produced a little bad feeling, for the insular Caroline insisted on calling it Pope Joan and playing it English version. Then the uproar would penetrate to the *salon*, and Michel or Monsieur would come forth to be stern.

"Though what they want quietness for beats me," Caroline said, "because as far as I can make out, whenever we watch, Madame always goes Three No-trumps, regardless, and then plays at such a rate that none of the others knows what she's doing."

But by day Michel was mostly with them, and they would take Michel's car down to St. Brioc to do the shopping for Madame or spend long, lazy afternoons at the *grève*. He was a marvellous swimmer, was Michel, and showed them all sorts of fancy strokes and dives. Caroline nearly burst her lungs trying to swim under water as long as he did, but he told her it took years of practice, and would himself come to the surface in the most unexpected places, right under Sara's nose as often as not, which was none too good for her poor nerves. It was much more fun when he bobbed up and tipped Raymond out of his canoe, apologising just as beautifully as if it had been an accident.

One day, some friends of Madame were calling in the afternoon, so Michel said he didn't feel social and what about a little excursion to St. Quay? "There is a *patisserie*"—with a twinkle at Sara—"and there is a *piscine* where we can bathe even when the tide's out, so even though it's busy and not at all a smart place, shall we go?"

Caroline and Sara felt that as they weren't used to Cannes standards they wouldn't be fussy, and agreed enthusiastically.

To St. Quay it was only about eight kilos, Michel told them.

"Five miles," Sara said proudly, having borrowed a pencil and worked it out, but it was a nerve-racking five miles for her, for she never could get used to the French habit of driving on the wrong side of the road. She had the full benefit of the front seat, too, being given that place of honour beside Michel, as the favourite. The road was good and Michel drove very fast and the agony of hurtling round corners on the right-hand side, feeling perfectly certain every minute of a head-on collision, made her shut her eyes tight and grip the seat in sheer terror.

Once in the town, she recovered sufficiently to open her eyes.

"Oh, *look*, Caro!" she bounced in her seat with excitement, "Two battleships in the bay!"

"Yes," muttered Caroline coldly. "Michel mentioned 'em to you about ten minutes ago, but you seemed to have gone into a trance or something."

Sara shot a hasty, embarrassed glance at Michel. How dreadful if he should realise she was scared of his beautiful driving, and think she wasn't enjoying herself, after his being so kind and everything! But Michel only smiled at her and asked:

"Sara, then, like the Navy?"

"Oh, yes!" Sara agreed fervently. "I love it—always sailing about having adventures and things. I'm going to marry a sailor when I'm old."

"No sensible sailor would have you, young or old." Caroline was not encouraging.

"Well, these are French sailors, so perhaps they will be safe from you," Raymond mocked her.

Michel created the now necessary diversion. "What are we going to do?" he said. "Bathe—visit the fleet, or a bit of it—have *goûter*——?"

"Lovely," agreed Caroline; "but can't we leave the fleet out?"

"Oh, gosh, Caro——"

"*Ma petite*," Michel soothed, "she is only drawing your leg." And Sara was so relieved to know she was not to be denied a closer acquaintance with the French Navy, that she quite forgot to laugh at Michel's slang.

They parked the car, and were soon in the *piscine*, an artificial pool built among the rocks where the girls found plenty to divert them. They derived endless amusement from the apparent passion of the men for wearing bathing-caps, while the sight of two rotund little Frenchmen, complete with caps and pointed beards, disporting themselves like sleek porpoises in the shallow end reduced them to their not infrequent state of giggles, aggravated by Raymond's complete inability to see anything in the least funny about them.

But the sight of Michel, from the dizzy top of the diving erection, making an exquisite swallow-dive filled them with envy.

"The first platform doesn't look so bad," said Caroline, eyeing it. "Let's try it."

"Right-oh," Sara agreed, ready for anything, and secretly rather proud of her diving. "Coming, Raymond?"

"I do not like to dive so high," answered Raymond firmly. "I shall watch you make the big splash, and laugh."

On the platform, Sara took one look at the pool below, and felt sick.

"Seems higher from here, doesn't it?" she said brightly, and sat down, looking round at the sea, the line of bathing-huts, the cliffs, the town—anywhere but at the water, all those miles beneath her.

"It'll be all right—I expect." Caroline's usually calm voice sounded a little breathless, but Sara was much too worried to notice.

"Oh, gosh, it's awful!" she thought. "And I hate heights, too. It's *miles*. Standing there, waiting to dive, looking at it—and I can't just *jump*, I'd look such a fool after climbing away up here." She was oblivious to the fact that Caroline seemed in no great hurry to move, leaning up against the wooden support, enjoying the view also. At last, however, she jumped up.

"Come on, Sara! Will you go first, or shall I?"

"Oh, you go!"

"Right. Tell me if I keep my legs straight," and she was gone.

Sara took one last agonized look at the water, shut her eyes and followed. She seemed to drop for hours, but finally she hit the water with a wallop, and came up to the surface, alive.

"My head's buzzing," she yelled at Caroline.

"So's mine," Caroline replied, as they swam vaguely round, dodging Michel's repeated arrivals. "Two pretty rotten dives, if you ask me." She paused, and added a second later, "Sara, I was terrified."

"Gosh, Caroline darling, I was *petrified*, but I thought you weren't minding so I didn't dare say a word."

"Sara."

"'Mm?"

"We'll have to do it again, just to show we're not, really."

"I know. Isn't it foul? Come on." With a companion in fear it did not seem so shattering the second time, and a third time was declared unnecessary to prove their courage.

"We'll be high-diving champions, soon," Sara suggested with her wonted optimism.

Michel and Raymond had gone down to the sea, and the girls raced over the sand after them; and then they dressed and went to secure places in a *vedette* going out to the ships.

"Which, Sara—*L'Hirondelle* or *Le Tonnerre*?"

"*L'Hirondelle* of course."

The entire population of St. Quay seemed to

share Sara's passion for the Navy, but finally they squeezed into a *vedette* which, what with over-crowding and Sara bouncing about, was in imminent danger of capsizing. Sara was so thrilled she had even put on her specs so that she should miss nothing.

An awkward ladder safely mounted, they found themselves at last on board. There were a few sailors about, one swabbing the deck.

"Which should have been done earlier, and not in the middle of the afternoon, I should have thought. And visitors about, too," Caroline remarked. "I'd like to see our Navy going on like that." Sara's elbow was digging into her ribs, a habit she heartily disliked, but of which she had so far failed to break her.

"They've got bare feet," Sara was saying, in an awed whisper. "How awful for them. And red bobbles on their caps—fun! Caro, I simply must take a photo of that one with the mop-thing."

Sara was an enthusiastic but unfortunate photographer. If she ever got anywhere near a proper focus, and had included both the victim's head and feet, she was usually too excited to keep her hand steady, and would move the camera violently as she pressed the trigger. A long series of lost cameras, besides, had proved too much for the family exchequer, but a misguided uncle had given her a midget one before she left for France, with the idea that its being small enough to go into her pocket, allowed some small hope of its staying there. And so it had done, Sara now usually forgetting all about it until it was too late.

However, here was a wonderful chance of local colour, and she dropped on to her knees, lest she should cut off that high-light of interest, the sailor's feet. Everything was beautifully arranged when a great dark shadow moved across her view-finder, and a cold voice from above said:

"It is not permitted, Mademoiselle. Give me your camera, if you please."

Sara looked up, rather crossly, into the stern face of a young officer, and was just about to start on one of her interminable arguments when Caroline quietly removed the offending camera and handed it over.

"I call that stealing," Sara grumbled in English. "Don't I get it back?" she demanded.

"When you leave the ship it will give me great pleasure to return it to you." His reply was polite, but firm, and Sara perforce had to give in.

But the incident had gained her a friend after all, for the officer relenting, and probably realising she would be safe where he could keep his eye on her, offered his august services as guide, which,

Michel and Raymond having wandered off on their own somewhere, the girls were only too glad to accept—as graciously as Sara's French permitted.

He did his job thoroughly, giving them long and technical descriptions of guns and routine which were quite over their heads, and which Sara constantly interrupted with a battery of questions of a more personal nature—did he like being in the Navy? Who darned his socks? Was he married? Had he any children? Where were they now?—until the poor man, who found this interest very flattering, suggested taking her below to show her photographs of his little ones.

"I'll wait for you on deck," said Caroline, rather bored, "and don't be long."

Sara reappeared, certainly, but there was by now such a great crush of people trying to get into the last *vedette* that Caroline did not notice her darting off again with a murmured "Gosh, my camera!" and as she herself had the misfortune to land with her full weight on the toe of an irate French matron, and was obliged to spend the next few minutes in a vain endeavour to mollify her, she did not have time to look round for Sara until the *vedette* was half-way to shore. Of course she was not there, and Caroline's agonized signals to Michel and Raymond, at the other end of the little boat, only met with uncomprehending smiles and nods.

"If you do not immediately cease to beat me with your arms, and trample me with your feet, Mademoiselle, I shall be obliged to retaliate," the erstwhile victim was saying frigidly, but with perfect courtesy, and Caroline subsided.

"I'll scrag that monkey when I get my hands on her," she vowed to herself. "Serve her right if the ship sails with her, and she's taken to North Africa or somewhere. I'll not go after her."

When the boat beached, she leaped out and got as far away from her fierce neighbour as possible before she unburdened herself to Michel.

"Sara's lost," she announced. "Oh, it's nothing to laugh at, Raymond—she's such an ass that there's no knowing what she will do! So please ask if there's another *vedette* going out, Michel."

But there wasn't, and the owner, with much waving of his arms, gave it as his opinion that it was absolutely impossible that a young English miss should have been left behind, that the deck had been as bare as the palm of his hand when they cast off, and that nothing, neither bribes nor threats, would induce him to go back on such a foolish errand. Raymond and Michel were thoroughly enjoying the argument, but Caroline was hot with embarrassment.

"Oh, do come away," she muttered, tugging at Michel's coat; "they'll bring the idiot back in one of the ship's boats."

But as Sara's new friend—M. Boyer was his name—was pointing out to Sara in great distress, the ship's cutter, and every other vessel, was ashore with men on afternoon leave, and there was no knowing when any of them would come back; although assuredly it would not be long, as the ship was due to sail for Brest at six o'clock.

Sara was thrilled. "Maybe there won't be time to get me off, and I'll have to come with you!" was her contribution to the discussion. M. Boyer looked rather alarmed at this; but thought as there was nothing to be done at the moment, he might be able to find her something to eat and some lemonade. So Sara, nothing loath, settled down to a good tuck-in of cakes, chocolate, peaches, and Grenadine syrup, while M. Boyer sat in amaze at the appetite of the so-small English schoolgirl. She told him, of course, that she wasn't English at all, but Scottish, although he showed the usual French incomprehension of the distinction.

"Ah yes, but I understand very well," he assured her; "I myself am a Breton." And Sara gave it up and talked of other things and ate, instead, and hoped the Captain wouldn't be cross when he came back and found her, and M. Boyer hoped so, too.

The shore party meantime had gone to the *pâtisserie*.

"There is no need to alarm yourself, Caroline," Michel comforted her; "we can see the landing-stage from here so we will go down whenever she arrives: no doubt they are waiting for a boat to bring her ashore." But although Caroline assured him she wasn't in the least upset she could not derive her usual enjoyment from a visit to a *pâtisserie*, chose cakes at random, and unfortunately picked on coffee éclairs which she didn't like much. She sipped her chocolate with a glum face.

"There's one thing," she said vindictively: "the brat will be sorry to miss tea." But Raymond laughed this consolation to scorn and declared that Sara would find something to eat in the middle of the Sahara.

"There's the ship's cutter going back," Michel broke in. They watched it out to *L'Hirondelle*, and saw it start back a little later. "She is not to be shanghaied this trip, then. If you two have eaten enough, we shall go down and claim our little lost one."

Sara, arriving in state with Lieutenant Boyer and no less a personage than the Captain himself, was grinning all over her face and no end pleased with herself. The Captain handed her ashore and with many bows and exchanges of compliments delivered her to her friends.

"We were desolated not to be able to keep her," he told Michel, and M. Boyer, who by this time was Sara's slave, muttered respectful—seeing his Captain was listening—but hearty agreement.

"Funny! We're jolly well desolated at getting you back, fathead," Caroline informed her as they walked up the beach to the car. Sara opened her green eyes wide.

"Darlings, you're not *cross!* It was a marvellous adventure, stranded on a French man-o'-war, and I had, gosh—such a tea! Peaches and——" on went the list as Raymond raised an eyebrow at the disgusted Caroline.

"And they were sweet. They honestly wanted to take me to Brest, but they thought it wouldn't be proper," she finished smugly.

Caroline snorted, Michel laughed and Raymond teased, but Sara settled into the car very happily. And from that day she has been a fervent supporter of the French Navy, and has incidentally set herself up as no little authority on it into the bargain.

CHAPTER VI

SHRIMPING

EVER since Raymond had pointed them out to her—a dim outline on the horizon—from the cliff above the *grève*, the very thought of the islands had fascinated Sara, and her imagination, never unfertile, was stirred by those mysterious bare rocks which only became visible at low tide.

"*Anything* in the way of adventures might happen on such exciting islands," she enthused to Caroline.

"The most exciting thing will be if you go and get left behind again, and drown yourself," Caroline replied—rather unnecessarily, Sara considered. "But are we actually going there?"

"Yes, rather. *La pêche* is a most important occasion. We start at all hours of the morning, Raymond told me, and stay all day, picnic and that, and we go after things called *crevettes*. Raymond didn't know the English name, nor did I. Here, have you got your wee dictionary? Lemme see—*co*—*cr*—here we are—*crevette*, *n.f.* shrimp!"

"Help! Are we going to hunt shrimp? How

exciting, Sara! How adventurous! And *when* does this thrill take place?"

"Shut up, you funny ass! I hope a shrimp turns on you and savages you, and that I, at the risk of my life, only shoot it down in the nick of time. Or maybe I won't bother. I don't know when we're going—we have to wait till the tide's right I suppose, and anyway it'll be fun. Shrimping's a thing I've never done, and there'll be the sail and the picnic."

Caroline looked even more doubtful. She was a bad sailor and, she suspected, a still worse shrimper, and altogether the expedition sounded to her like one of Madame's less happy thoughts.

But meantime the tide apparently stayed wrong and the days slipped by, cloudless, hot and full of the magic of strange sights and sounds. To the Scots, used at the best, to one sunny day followed by six grey ones, the unbroken succession of perfect days was a revelation. Every morning (and Sara sometimes felt that this was the very best moment of the whole happy day) to find the sun shining in their wide-open, unshuttered window, and making even more gay their patch-work coverlets, came as a little shock of pleasure. Until Louise or Yvonne appeared with breakfast Sara, who always woke long before Caroline, would lie and think of the sun, and the funny

French smells, and the funny French ways; all the nice things that happened yesterday and all the exciting adventures that were going to happen to-day. Most often, she would hop out of bed and get her sewing, for she could never bear to be still for long: and Louise's greeting was an amazed, "Sewing already, Mademoiselle?" Only with the good smell of coffee would Caroline show signs of life.

But on the morning of *la pêche*, the tide having been defeated at last, the usual comfortable lazy morning routine was shattered. They were called at five, while it was still quite dark, swallowed *petit déjeuner* in the dining-room, standing, Raymond wildly excited at the thought of getting into a boat again and chattering sixteen to the dozen, Michel rather monosyllabic and a suitable companion for Caroline, who was quite strenuously hating the whole business, and looked it, while Sara was, of course, excited too and annoyingly bright. Monsieur and Madame were at the door, piling the wagonette with picnic basket, bathing things, nets, fishing-tackle, coats—and it finally rolled off, Madame and Monsieur perched rather insecurely on top of the whole conglomeration, while the others walked down the cliff path to St. Brioc.

It was light now, and as they descended the sun

came up through the trees, and the sight of it, and the fat, pink clouds melting quickly away, cheered even Caroline. The goats were up and about too, rattling their chains and getting in the way as usual: and Raymond went bouncing down the path with much more abandon than any goat.

They reached the harbour as soon as the wagon-ette and went along the quay to the spot, almost at the lighthouse, where the boat was waiting. Raymond left them immediately, and began discussing wind and tides with Maturin *père*, a stocky little fisherman with a blue jersey, and a twinkle in his eye, who was to take them across. Maturin *fils* was introduced too, but it was decided to leave him behind as Maturin *père* and Raymond could easily manage the boat between them. *Le Coquelicot* itself, which was brown, with a sail as red as its namesake, delighted Sara, and would normally have appealed to Caroline's eye too, but a good fresh breeze was filling her with alarm which left her little interest in the picturesque.

After much talk and many a false start, they and all the odds and ends were safely stowed away, and Maturin *père* rowed them out of the harbour. Not in a normal way, but with one oar, stuck through a hole in the stern, which he waggled from side to side with great energy; and success too, for, contrary to the expectations of Caroline, who didn't think much of this outlandish fashion of rowing, they made excellent progress.

Once out in the open sea, Raymond was in his element, blind and deaf to everyone and everything except the boat and Maturin, leaping about, pulling now on this rope and now on that, shouting at Maturin *père*, who shouted back. There was indeed a wind strong and dead against them, and so, although the islands were no great distance, they had to tack up-wind for hours.

Little white horses pranced on the blue sea, and Michel and Sara climbed right on to the bow, where they sat, drenched with spray, and sang at the tops of their voices; and Sara gave them sea-shanties, all she knew—which was quite a considerable number, as her singing mistress at school had had a great passion for them last term.

Caroline put on a big coat and huddled as near the middle of the boat as she could judge—not that it made much difference, Sara casting an occasional glance at her, filled with all the good sailor's pity and contempt for the weaker vessel. She did jump down once to see if Caroline were really ill.

"Oh, angel," she said, "your face is exactly the colour of your coat." As the coat was Caroline's bottle-green school one she felt that if that was all Sara had come to say she might as well have stayed where she was.

However, Caroline had her revenge. After sailing some three hours or so, as the boat drew nearer the islands so Sara's hearty singing became less hearty, and no sooner had she clambered into the rowing-boat with the others than the worst happened. Not that Sara's was the usual complaint.

"This isn't sea-sickness," she thought. "It couldn't be. Gosh, this is awful: this is some frightful disease! I'm going to die. . . . I wish I *could* die."

But death, somehow, stayed his hand, though it was two rather limp girls who set foot on the islands. *Mal de mer* didn't come within the experience of either Monsieur or Raymond so they didn't even notice anything was amiss. Michel was the essence of tact and refrained from teasing; Madame was full of solicitude, and prophesied that in five minutes, five little minutes only, all would be well again.

And so it proved; and as Madame laid the food in the shade of a rock, Monsieur handed out the nets. Raymond and Michel went off on a fierce expedition after crab, armed with nets and sharp-pronged instruments.

Caroline accepted her net as if it were a loaded gun over which she had little or no control.

"What do I do with this thing?" she demanded, holding it at arm's length and eyeing it with distaste.

"Oh, shrimp, of course!" Sara, never at a loss, made a large and vague gesture, catching Monsieur a nasty crack on the head.

"*Tiens*, Mademoiselle! Do you think I am a shrimp that you catch me in your net?" he wanted to know. "Look, take this basket for your spoils."

Caroline was feeling that no spoils of hers would ever find their way into the basket when Sara, hastily putting on her specs, nudged her and whispered, "Better see what Madame does. Look——" They covertly watched Madame shove her net into one of the little sea-weedy pools which seemed to be all over the rocky islands, lift it out, put simply handfuls of something into her basket and then start the performance all over again.

"I say," said Sara, "what does a shrimp look like, Caro? I've—er—forgotten."

"Well, it's pink." Caroline's voice was dubious. "But we never have them at home, because Mummy loathes fishy things."

"No, neither do we. *How* they neglect our

education. Well, come on—we'll dip our nets in,
and look for something pink. And maybe we'll
find some pearls, too!" she added.

The islands, sun-bathed masses of rock, covered
in their lower parts with pools and stretches of
sea-weed, seemed to have attracted many people
besides the Petit Chose party. Scattered here and
there, queer figures slowly wandered, with skirts
hitched up into ungainly bunches or with
trousers rolled, bent silently over their nets as if
celebrating some mystic rite. The two girls, in
bathing-dresses and shorts, looked very workman-
like, while the stout rope soles of their *espadrilles*
protected their feet and prevented their slipping,
at the same time allowing them to splash where-
ever they had a mind. But their ineffectual pokes
with their nets, their squeals and giggles, made
many a true shrimper glance at them in consternation.

"Look at this lot, Caroline," said Sara, her nose
practically touching the net in her eagerness to
locate something which might possibly be
regarded as a shrimp. "Sea-weed, shells, things
like minnows, wee squirmers, sort of jelly-fish, all
transparent. Not a trace of pink."

"Sara—of course! I'm crackers! Maybe the
beastly things aren't born pink—but go pink in
the pot—like lobster——"

"Some are born pink—and some have pinkness thrust upon them——" Sara murmured fatuously —showing incidentally her first and only sign of acquaintance with last term's Shakespeare. But she suddenly woke up.

"Caroline, nobody would ever suspect it, but you're a genius really. Those transparent things with the lots of legs—shrimps, I'll bet! Disguised, the cads, to make it more difficult for us. We'll swallow our pride and ask Madame."

Madame was nowhere to be seen, but a total stranger, an earnest female with a long thin nose, was—there she stood, pushing handfuls of something into her basket.

The two went over to her, and Sara extracted one of the slippery amœba-like creatures from her net, not without considerable reluctance on its part.

"*Crevette?*" she queried, with one of her nicest, she couldn't help feeling, smiles.

"*Mais, oui!*" The woman looked amazed, as well she might, and hastened away as fast as the rough going would let her, from these, no doubt dangerous, lunatics who came to a famous shrimping-ground, dressed for shrimping, armed for shrimping, and yet not knowing a shrimp when they saw one.

"Horrid creature!" said Sara ungratefully; "she

had that 'Fancy not knowing that' look in her
eye people are so fond of turning on me. But
anyway, things are certainly looking brighter
now," she finished. And even Caroline had to
admit that once they knew what they were after,
shrimping was rather fun; they became as ardent
shrimp-fans as the lady with the long nose, and
very soon had a fairly creditable show in their
basket, so that when Raymond came leaping over
the rocks to ask if lunch didn't interest them at all,
they were both sorry to stop.

Madame's way with a picnic was quite simple.
She filled huge baskets with pies, with jars of
foie-gras, with cold ham and veal, with a crock
of butter, with cakes from the *pâtisserie*, with
fruit and with a jar of the home-brewed cider
which was the staple drink at Petit Chose and
which Caroline hated; pointed loaves, as long as
your arm, had been added in the village, and now,
as the girls approached the flat pebbly bit of
beach where the dinghy was beached and the food
spread, she was clutching one of them to her
chest, hacking at it unmercifully with a mur-
derous-looking knife. Monsieur and Michel were
already well under way, and Michel waved a
welcoming piece of bread at the two, who,
suddenly realising that they hadn't seen food for
hours, and were simply ravenous, found no fault

with a picnic definitely superior, as Sara affirmed, to lots of niggling little sandwiches which blow you up at the time, but have no lasting effect. . . .

Sara, finally, languidly, brushed a few, a very few crumbs off herself and stretched out on the pebbles, the hot sun beating down on her until she simply had to close her eyes, just for a minute . . . just . . . for . . . a . . . minute . . . or two. . . .

Raymond and the men went off again on the great crab-hunt, but Madame, whose groaning basket of shrimps had brought the blush of shame to the girls' cheeks, leaned back against a rock and prepared to be lazy. Caroline, much too well fed to be otherwise, also made herself as comfortable as the somewhat unresponsive beach would let her and, never at the best very fluent in the French tongue, cast round rather helplessly for a topic of conversation which wouldn't involve either much effort on her part or a very varied vocabulary. Her eyes thankfully lighted on Maturin, stolidly but with evident enjoyment eating his own lunch in the rowing-boat.

"Maturin *père* has a kindly air, Madame," she ventured.

"Ah yes, Caroline," Madame replied, "he has indeed. We are all devoted to the Maturins, you understand. You see, a very long time ago, in the Revolution, it was an ancestor of Maturin's who helped our ancestors to escape."

"Oh, Madame, not really? How thrilling!" Even the calmness of Caroline was disturbed. "Tell me about it, please, would you? Was it exciting?"

"But certainly it was exciting. You must know that Petit Chose was not built till after the Revolution—all that remains of the former great Château de St. Brioc is that ruin in the trees behind the tennis-court——"

"Oh, yes, Raymond did say something about that when Sara asked him—sorry, Madame, please go on."

"Well, then. My ancestor—he is mine as well as my husband's because we are very distantly related—was Hubert, Marquis de St. Brioc, a nasty old creature, to be honest, and a cruel land-lord to his tenants. His only son, Hubert, was not like him, but a fine young man whom many of the villagers had come to love although they hated his father; and he lived in the Château with his little wife Antoinette and his uncle Philippe, a great scholar, who studied mediæval literature or something of the sort—Caroline, is it necessary to throw stones on to Sara's stomach?"

"Yes, truly it is, Madame—she would never

forgive me if she missed this story, and I didn't want to interrupt you."

"You are so kind, Caroline, but I would rather be interrupted than receive one of your misdirected missiles on my nose. Waken the little one, then."

So Sara, rather cross, was wakened, but when she heard what it was all about she squeaked with excitement and settled down to enjoy herself. They listened, as Madame told the story in her clear, soft voice. The language not their own, with words sometimes only half-understood, seemed to give it an added atmosphere of strangeness and gloom, and the bright sun on the water and the warm friendly rocks faded, and they saw instead the dark night of terror, the unhappy ignorant mob, inflamed with emotions of rage and hatred they could scarcely understand, far less control, hastening, pushing, jostling up the cliff paths, guarding all ways of escape; and those others in the Château, helpless, being surrounded by men to whom no appeal had any meaning, men suddenly become no longer human.

"It was the Maturin *fils* of that day who warned them that the peasants were approaching. He with his father were among the very few loyal ones, and he too knew of the passage, made years and years before, which led from the Château to a cove in a lonely part of the shore. Maturin *père* took his fishing-boat round the headland to the little cove and Maturin *fils* hurried to the Château. But M. le Marquis de St. Brioc refused to leave his home: no despised peasant was going to frighten him away. He ordered Philippe and his son and daughter-in-law to go, and since in any case Antoinette could not go alone, they had to obey. They gathered what valuables they could carry, and with Maturin *fils* escaped by the secret passage. The boat was waiting and the Maturins sailed them to England."

There was a long pause. Then Sara sighed a gusty sigh. "Poor, poor things!" she said; "but I'm glad they got safely to England."

"Safely to England, yes," said Madame, "but alas!—grief and excitement and the formidable cold of the journey in the boat must have been too much for the poor scholar, for he died immediately after their arrival. It is his ghost"— Madame's voice, as became a true daughter of Brittany, dropped a little—"which haunts the little cove."

"Oh, Madame!" Sara's green eyes were very nearly out of her head. "You've got a real live *ghost* in the family, and you never told me! How *marvellous*! Have you seen him? Does he appear?"

Madame, ignoring, like Sara, Caroline's grunts and smiles of scepticism, seemed to take these questions quite seriously.

"Ah, but yes, he appears—in a long black travelling cloak—although I have never seen him. My brother—he was killed in the War—saw him twice. And that is the reason we never use the little cove for bathing; the peasants will not go near it, nor our Breton servants either, of course. Nor will anything induce them to approach the ruin, although Philippe has never actually been seen there——"

"I know what it is," Sara broke in, her imagination working overtime since her little nap: "poor Philippe left some frightfully valuable treasure behind and his spirit comes back to haunt the place until it shall be found. Madame—*have* you searched all that passage?"

Madame laughed. "I am desolated to disappoint you, my poor Sara, but I fear all the real valuables which could be carried went to England, for my ancestors came back to France, quite wealthy, some years later."

"What happened to the wicked old Marquis?" demanded Caroline with rather gloomy relish.

"Ah, *he* came by the fate he doubtless deserved," Madame continued the story. "The revolutionaries put him to death—no, I do not know in what manner, Sara—and set fire to the Château. When young Hubert and Antoinette came back to France they built Petit Chose—a little thingummy, a trifle, they thought it and called it. And so, Sara, no one bothered about the ruined Château and the secret passage. Now no one knows, even, where it started from; and as a fall of rock many years ago blocked the approach from the cave, it has vanished—pouf!" And Madame snapped her fingers, dismissing it. Sara looked as if all her dearest hopes had been suddenly dashed.

"Gosh, isn't that *miserable*," she mourned, "to go and lose a lovely, thrilling secret passage, full of adventures——"

"Full of rocks, you mean. It was probably a horrid, gloomy hole, anyway—but I should have liked to explore it." Caroline's tone was a little wistful, too. "Of course," she brightened, "there is still the cave. . . .

"Yes," she continued later, when, the goodly haul of crab and shrimp, and themselves bundled into *Le Coquelicot*, they were scudding homewards before the wind. "Yes, Sara my cherub, what about exploring the cave to-morrow? It's in that little bay we saw from the cliff one night."

"Well," Sara sounded doubtful, "it's Michel's last day, and we have all sorts of dates with him—

tennis in the morning, if we get the court cleared, that is—and bathing—and I don't suppose he would care about exploring a cave——"

"All right, all right. The next day?"

"We-ell——" Sara began, even more doubtfully. Caroline turned from her contemplation of the fast receding islands and stared at her.

"What's the matter with you? Lovely cave full of adventures and ghosts—oh, ho! That's it, is it? You wouldn't let a poor old ghost stop you having adventures, would you?"

"Course I wouldn't, silly fathead. I'm not frightened, not a bit, only—only it's no use stirring up trouble—you don't believe in ghosts, but I do."

"And with reason." Michel had evidently been listening, having become bored trying to sail the boat under Raymond's ferocious instructions. "But Philippe is a very gentle spirit, Sara. Look," he went on, "we have almost arrived."

"Did you enjoy the fishing, Caroline?" Monsieur inquired as they disembarked.

"Yes, very much, Monsieur, thank you," Caroline decided definitely after thought.

"I loved it," Sara breathed rapturously. "I'm going to empty out our wonderful catch on to the quay and photograph it. "Where's our basket, Caro?"

"Well, you had it when we were leaving the islands," Caroline answered. "Didn't you put it in the boat?" she added in a hopeless sort of voice.

"Gosh, I thought I did—but I was talking to Raymond at the time and——"

Raymond gave a sudden guffaw as the absurdity of the tragedy struck him.

"Poor Sara!" He patted her sympathetically on the shoulder. "For days and days we plan this expedition, we sail for hours on a cruel sea, we break our backs to fish—all in order that you may get those shrimps. And in the end you leave them for the tide to come and take back, basket and all!"

CHAPTER VII

THE FOURTEENTH OF JULY

THEY were sitting in the *salon* next morning, Sara and Caroline and Madame. Caroline was reluctantly writing home—"Dearest Mummy and Daddy, I am very well and still enjoying myself. Learning French like anything. We went shrimping yesterday, but Sara left our shrimps behind. Raymond has just fallen over Ajax again—what a hullabaloo. Could I have some money, do you think? Love from Sara and me, Caroline."

The said Sara was giving a spirited rendering of *Au Clair de la Lune* on the piano with one finger. Madame had just resumed her embroidery after having administered first-aid to Raymond and the loudly complaining Ajax. Outside, the gardener and a rather vacant-looking youth from the farm were clearing the tennis-court of the foot-deep mould of last year's leaves with long brooms made of twigs, while Monsieur and Michel shouted conflicting instructions which completely upset the vacant-looking youth; and Raymond, not having learned his lesson, still further added to the confusion by leaping about, though rather lamely after his recent encounter with Ajax and the *salon* floor, getting in the way of the brooms.

"To-day," Madame suddenly announced, dramatically, "is the Fourteenth of July!"

Sara looked up from her music, losing her place, but with no apparent difference in the sounds issuing from the tortured piano.

"Oh? Somebody's birthday?" she said, brightly.

Caroline turned a cold eye on her, and Madame, rather scandalized, said even more dramatically, "The Birthday of the French Republic!"

"Fall of the Bastille, fathead," Caroline threw at the pianist. Sara, still vague, regarded her admiringly.

"I don't know where you learn these things, Caroline. What happens, Madame? Fun and games?"

"Nothing very much, here in St. Brioc, really," Madame answered. "Every one has a holiday, and to-night in the village there is a *Bal de Nuit.* I thought we might go down and watch for a very little while, if that would amuse you."

"Lovely, lovely!" Sara agreed, and gleefully told Michel the news as he came in to announce the court more or less cleared and would they like a game of tennis? Caroline was good, for her age, remarkably good at tennis, and sped upstairs to change her shoes and fetch a racquet; Sara, who could not, simply could not, hit a moving object, thought she would rather not play. She was to regret that decision bitterly before long, for as the court had no outside netting and the balls were constantly getting lost among the surrounding trees she was given the job of ball-boy, a heart-breaking business, especially for one whose eye-sight was not of the best. As a matter of fact, every now and then the game had perforce to stop, while the whole party took to the woods to search for balls. This light-hearted tennis-cum-hunt-the-thimble was all rather upsetting for poor Caroline, who took her tennis seriously, but when they were actually on the court she enjoyed herself, though Monsieur, a rather slow but painstaking player, and Raymond, stylish, flashy and definitely erratic, were no match for her and Michel, who was a master.

"What a blow, you're going away to-morrow," she grumbled to him as they went in to lunch. "I've never had a chance to play with any one so good before."

"You shall come and play on my court in Cannes one day," he promised her, "but you must practise that fore-hand drive first!"

"Can I come, too, if I practise my fore-hand drive?" Sara, who liked to be in on everything, chipped in. Caroline, knowing Sara's tennis,

scoffed, but Michel assured her rather flamboy-
antly that there would be a welcome for her even
if she played the worst game of tennis in the
world.

"I do!" Sara giggled into her soup-plate,
highly gratified.

They bathed in the afternoon. The *grève*, as a
rule inhabited only by themselves, was "thick
with people"—Sara's phrase, spoken as they lay
in the shallow water splashing with their feet.
"Gosh, half St. Brioc seems to be here! But aren't
the old dears sweet in their stiff coifs?"

"'Mm. Different districts have a different
style, so Madame told me. Terribly snow-white,
aren't they? Help! What's this?"

"This," was Raymond, in a bathing-costume,
mounted on a staid old farm-horse, urging it to
prance into the sea, encouraged by the shouts
of the admiring villagers who like every one else
knew and doted on Raymond.

"I'm going to swim her across to England," he
cried, "or at least to St. Brioc, or out to Michel,"
waving his arm to the distant speck which was
Michel. But Coquette, singularly inappropriate
name for such a dignified matron, had other
plans, for throwing up her staid old heels she
deposited her burden in the water, and lumbered
back up the beach to her delighted owner.

"So the great Raymond, the best rider in Paris, has met his match, has he?" Michel swam up and mocked him. "Look, Coquette does not throw the farm children!" For Coquette, her skittishness forgotten, was allowing herself to be led home by the farmer, under a goodly load of young Jeans and Yvonnes and Sylvestres, not to mention a huge basket of the fragments of the day's picnic.

"Do you ride much, then?" Caroline asked in innocent surprise.

Michel laughed. "He adores horses, and rides anything with four legs, not always, as you see, with success."

Whatever Sara, and to a less extent, Caroline, who seldom wasted her time visualizing any situation before she came face to face with it, had imagined the *Bal de Nuit* would be like, they were quite unprepared for the reality. When they arrived (Sara rather jaundiced through having been forced to abandon her projected third helping of chocolate pudding at dinner) the ball was well started, the ice, if there ever had been any, long since melted. In the middle of the market square, under the sky, the band, consisting solely of fiddles and accordions, two of each, were standing on a little raised platform working away manfully. Round them, on the bare hard soil of

France, the inhabitants of St. Brioc danced.
Most of the women wore their snowy caps, some
had embroidered aprons over their long black
dresses and little embroidered shawls round their
shoulders; the men were in their dark fishing
jerseys and flat felt hats or berets with here and
there a dandy in more townified garments. They
were singing:

> " *Gibouli, giboula,*
> *Où dit qu'elle est malade*
> *Gibouli, giboula,*
> *Où dit qu'elle va mourir.*"

and in spite of the mournful nature of the words,
it had a fine, rollicking tune, and they hopped
first on one foot then on the other, and finally
did a little jig round.

"Oh, I could do that!" cried Sara, hopping
already in sympathy. Madame gave them a
special demonstration, and very soon the Petit
Chose party were jigging round with the best of
them, while Sara and Caroline weren't long in
finding that to sing and dance *that* dance at the
same time was an exhausting business. When at
long last the band took pity and stopped, they
leaned against each other and panted. And when
the musicians as a concession to progress struck
up what they called a fox-trot but which they
played at three times the orthodox speed, the two

collected Raymond, feeling they should wander off to get a little nourishment at a sweet-stall Caroline had spotted as she jigged.

"I'm very fond of nougat," Sara confided to the amazed young woman, who had never had such a customer. "Nice name for sweeties, *Pierrot Gourmand*." When she finally decided she had laid in enough for the evening, they turned away, cheeks and pockets bulging, and then Raymond, who was everywhere at once and seemed to have a hundred eyes, spotted a further object of interest.

"Look! Over there——"

Sara, vainly peering in quite the wrong direction out to sea—her glasses having been pushed into her blazer pocket when she started *Gibouli, Giboula*—was muttering, "I don't see *anything*——"

"*There*, blind bat," Caroline swung her round and pointed: "it's a circus."

Sure enough, from a big round tent well to one side of the square came suddenly gales of laughter and clapping.

"Oh, let's go there!" said Sara.

"It is too late to-night," Raymond replied; "we'll come to-morrow. But let's go round the back and see what's to be seen."

Caroline guided Sara past the many taut ropes, traps for unwary feet, holding the Big Top in position, until they could see the artistes' entrance, all a-bustle with performers, clowns with their ridiculous clothes and more ridiculous faces, patient animals and not so patient humans, stout equestriennes and slim acrobats skipping in, their fixed smiles ready, coming thankfully out, mopping their brows.

It was Raymond who discovered the ponies, four of them, snow-white, resting in their loose boxes in a quiet corner, their turn either finished, or not yet begun.

"Aren't they darlings?" Sara said, as one nuzzled at her gently. "I like you," she told him; "and you've got your name on the door—*Perce-neige*—what's that mean, Raymond?"

"Snowdrop," supplied Caroline.

"Gosh, look, isn't he clever? He's nosing round my pocket—bet he smells that nougat! Very well, old boy, you shall have some. Oh, it's all right, Caro, nougat's terribly good for horses, isn't it, Raymond?" But Raymond, busy petting one of the other ponies and not paying much attention to Sara's chatter, never had a chance to give his expert opinion, for Sara had the stick of nougat out of its paper and into Snowdrop's mouth before he could see what she was up to.

"Christopher! He soon put that away!" Sara was charmed to find a fellow nougat-fancier, albeit a dumb one. Not so dumb all the same that he couldn't make clear that he was ready for more of the delicious stuff, the like of which had never come his way before. But as the fourth stick disappeared, Caroline thought it was time someone curbed Sara's misguided generosity.

"Oh, shut up feeding him, Sara!" she exhorted, without heat, "You've probably ruined him for life. Sugar breaks their wind or something—whatever that may mean." Caroline was no horsewoman. Sara pointed out, reasonably enough, that it wasn't sugar, but nougat. "And anyway," she went on virtuously, "their owner should be here looking after them and not be gallivanting off somewhere, while stray people come up and poison his ponies. I think he ought to be reported to the R.S.P.—what d'you call it?—if they have one in France which I doubt."

Caroline, rather rattled at the turn the argument had taken, and knowing Sara to be quite capable of seeking out the owner at his peaceful and doubtless well-earned supper, and giving him a good dressing-down for allowing her to feed his ponies on anything she fancied, hurriedly regained Raymond's attention and suggested they had better find Madame again.

"But it was fascinating the way he gobbled the stuff," Sara mused as they went back to collect Madame, who decided they had now seen enough of St. Brioc's night life and marched them off home. Caroline was still doubtful about the probable fate of Snowdrop's wind, but as Michel, on consultation, didn't seem to think one meal of nougat would do the pony much harm, she decided that she needn't upset herself any more.

Had she foreseen the sequel, even Caroline's monumental calm would have been shaken.

CHAPTER VIII

SARA AT THE CIRCUS

"Did you know," Caroline asked of Sara at break-fast next morning, carefully filling up the holes in her slice of bread with butter, "did you know that Raymond is supposed to be working for an exam. at the moment?"

"Raymond? Swotting? You're raving! Why, he has never opened a book since he came!"

"'Mm. He does disappear to his room some-times after Madame's had a word or two with him."

"Yes, but he's never gone more than half an hour, and he always takes the phonograph with him."

Caroline gave a sudden splutter of laughter. "Fat lot of work he'll do with that infernal machine within a mile of him," she observed. Since the day, long before the girls' acquaintance with it, that Raymond had in his exuberance sent the unfortunate gramophone flying off a table, it had in revenge refused to play unless wound almost constantly: six windings to a record were nothing to its insatiable innards, but

Raymond adored it and would not be parted from it.

"It's all rather rotten for him, really," Caroline went on. "Michel told me when we were struggling up that beastly path in the dark last night, with you and Raymond falling in and out of ditches and screaming the place down. Seems he's awfully keen on horses and all that and he wanted to join some crack cavalry regiment or other, but there isn't enough money, and so he has to go in for this—government job, I think Michel was trying to say. Like Papa, I suppose—he's something in the government. Hence the exam. He failed before, in March, and he's having another go in a day or two. Madame's terribly worried apparently."

"Gosh, Raymond doesn't seem to be! But it is rather sickening for him, and he's awfully good about it, Caro, now I come to think of it, never grumbles or anything. I believe I do remember him saying something about an exam, but I thought it would be at Christmas at the earliest from the casual way he mentioned it. Oh, gosh!" Sara's tender heart was stirred: "he'll loathe poking about in an office all day——"

"He'd wreck the place in a week," Caroline interrupted. "Look at the way he's always falling over Ajax and jumping the tennis net and leaping downstairs and knocking trays of dishes out of Louise's hands—she fairly ticked him off for that, all the same," and she chuckled at the memory.

"Yes," Sara was quite definite, "he'd be much safer stuck on a horse and he could leap walls and things. Gosh, Caroline, if we could only find old Philippe's treasure——"

"Your reading matter must have been even sillier than usual, and I thought you only read thrillers." Caroline was scornful. "Didn't you hear Madame? There *is* no treasure. And a fat chance of finding it you have when you won't even put your nose inside the cave!"

"Caroline, for Raymond's and Madame's sake, not to mention Papa, the pet, I'll dare all," Sara announced, waving an unfortunately full coffee-cup. "We'll go this very afternoon. Oh, no, of course," she added, rather quickly, mopping up the mess with a corner of the sheet, "Michel's leaving after lunch. Wouldn't be time, for we'll need early dinner if we're going to the circus. I shall miss that man, you know. We'll need the circus to cheer us up." . . .

But Madame had the strongest and most unwelcome views on the subject of all this gaiety, when Raymond put it to her as they were gathered in the *salon* after lunch, drinking the rather bitter French coffee, and waiting for the post to come in!

No, no, no, no—Raymond was mad, Raymond
was imbecile even to suggest such an eccentricity.
It was not so much the circus she minded, although
she had no doubt it would be very inferior and
that they would all contract some dreadful
disease, no, it was two such late nights running—
they would go home wrecks, pale, hollow-eyed,
these precious delicate girls.

The delicate girls gazed at her, Caroline with
faint distaste at the fuss, wondering why she
didn't just say no and shut up, Sara with all the
admiration of an ardent amateur of the art of
volubility for the stamp of the master. In fact
the only person who really wasn't listening at all
was Raymond, and he never let her suspect it:
he was well used to these outbursts, for his care-
less, casual gaiety often drove his mother dis-
tracted, on which occasions a great flow of words
would relieve her pent-up feelings; at her first
exhausted pause, Raymond would apologise very
charmingly and kiss her hand and she would
forgive him immediately.

This time the entry of Louise with the letters
created a diversion.

"One for Mademoiselle Caroline," she handed
them out, "two for Mademoiselle Sara—and you
owe Marie la Cuisinière four *sous*, Mademoiselle."

Sara stared at the handwriting furiously. "It's

that fat idiot Sausage, this time. Lend me four *sous*, Caro, there's an angel. How much do you reckon we've had to pay on letters with those miserable blighters not putting enough stamps on?"

"Pounds, I should think," said Caroline lugubriously.

"Pounds and pounds," Sara amplified, handing over the money to Louise who, with Marie la Cuisinière, the usual financer, thought the almost daily payments to the postman a huge joke, and was waiting hopefully for a parcel to arrive.

Michel came in just then, through the French window, having been seeing to his car, and hearing there was to be no visit to the circus suggested the two should see him on his way as far as St. Quay, and then take the little train back.

"I adore that little train," said Sara (it had taken them and Madame to St. Brieuc one day), "the way it meanders all over the countryside, through villages and along the roads. And the level-crossings! Don't they ever have any bridges in this country? They certainly don't seem ever to have platforms at their stations. But all the same, I think we should walk home—I'm getting horribly fat. And I must put on some other shoes if we do—I don't fancy walking eight kilos in *espadrilles*."

Madame, who would not have fancied walking one kilo, far less eight, in anything, thought this a bizarre idea, but knowing that these strange guests of hers apparently enjoyed walking for walking's sake, agreed willingly. Raymond politely declined to join them, and they hurried upstairs to change their shoes.

"My new brown-and-white ones, I think," said Sara, anxious to cut a dash.

"Better put some socks on—they'll be stiff," Caroline advised.

"Oh no, I couldn't bear the heat on those dusty roads," answered Sara. Caroline shrugged, and said no more.

Michel's affectionate farewells over, they set off on their rather sad little drive, for Michel had been fun, and they were sorry to lose him. But a specially large tea of chocolate with cream and quantities of rich delicious cakes revived their spirits somewhat, and they waved him on his way more cheerfully, amid promises to visit him at Cannes the very next holidays, and set off homewards.

They soon discovered that going for walks on French roads was an eccentricity firmly discouraged by the motorists. Cars approached at an incredible speed, and certain death was only to be avoided by scrambling up the steep bank at the side of the road and cowering there until the menace, with its attendant cloud of dust, should pass.

"If they'd only keep to the proper side of the road," Caroline muttered savagely after each one passed. "They're always attacking us where I don't expect them."

"Well, the poor things haven't had our advantages," said Sara smugly. "Oh, gosh, Caroline, you were right about those shoes,"—Sara had indeed begun to hobble rather alarmingly— "I'm sure I've got a blister. Could I take 'em off, do you think, and walk in my bare feet?"

"You could," Caroline replied. "You could also crawl on hands and knees, or walk on your hands and wave your feet in the air."

"Ass! You've no idea what I'm suffering."

"I shouldn't wonder but what you'll tell me sooner or later. But I'm not a bit sorry for you. You've no sense, that's what's the matter with you. Half crippled and you won't wear socks; half blind and you won't wear your specs—look at you now, peering at an old tree as if it was going to bite you."

"Tree? So it is!" Sara gave an embarrassed but relieved giggle. "And I thought it was a horrid old creature with a sack on his back who was probably coming over to murder us. Not that

I'd mind actually, because I'm in great pain. And you're a callous beast."

They reached St. Brioc at last, thankful to get off the road alive, bought a bag of peaches to comfort themselves, and finally got to Rest-and-be-thankful, a particular little grassy patch they had discovered beside the cliff path, where the hedge was broken and there was to be had a grand view of St. Brioc and out over the sea.

"It's a mercy peaches are so cheap or we'd have been ruined," Sara observed, finishing her fourth and flicking the stone at a too inquisitive goat who was showing a desire to take the very bite out of her mouth.

"You can see the circus from here," Caroline said lazily, lying on her stomach and gazing towards the still, sunlit village.

"One, two, three—get away, goat—nine, ten, *eleven*! Eleven blisters among ten toes!" Sara wailed. "Caroline, will I ever walk again?"

"Oh, I expect so!" Caroline rolled over and examined the damage interestedly. "Sore are they, little shrimp? Come on then, we'll get you home and bathe them. And d'you think we ought to let that goat eat the paper bag?"

Sara giggled. "That's carrying anti-litter too far, if you ask me, but goats eat anything."

"Obviously. Can you bear your shoes on

again? Off we go, then. You do like to keep a few blisters about you, I must say. . . ."

Sara's scars didn't prevent her setting off with Caroline and Raymond the next evening—after a very early dinner—for the circus, Raymond's wiles and the girls' obvious eagerness having prevailed over Madame's last lingering scruples.

"We must have the very front row," Raymond was insisting, hustling them unmercifully along the narrow lane near the house, when there was a rumbling and a rattling behind them and a great voice shouted:

"*Holà*, Monsieur Raymond! You are going to St. Brioc? Would you like a lift?" and Monsieur le Boulanger drew up his bread-cart with a flourish, beaming at them all over his round red face. They climbed up gratefully on to the wooden seat. The cart was high, with deep wooden sides within which the remaining loaves —long, thin ones and great round fat ones—were lying.

Monsieur le Boulanger, delighted to have their company and determined to show what his good little pony could do, drove down that road like a very Jehu. The noise was indescribable, for the cart had hard wheels and, as far as the passengers could discover, no springs, and they jolted over the rough and rutty lane in fine style, while behind them and under the seat the loaves hopped and danced merrily. Raymond and Monsieur le Boulanger conversed at the pitch of their voices— they had to—so that the peasants in the cottages they passed rushed to their doors to see what was ado.

"What a contraption!" yelled Caroline in Sara's ear, but she—with one hand hanging on to the seat for her life and the other frenziedly clutching the beret which Caroline, with some inexplicable and suddenly awakened idea of propriety, had forced on her reluctant head—for once had nothing to say.

They arrived, contrary to expectations, intact though indeed rather shattered, in plenty of time to lay in what Sara considered an adequate store of *Pierrot Gourmand* nougat, and to establish themselves right at the very ring-side, beside an aisle, Raymond in the middle and Sara next the passage.

Probably Caroline and Sara derived more amusement from the audience than from the circus itself, for the clowns' patter was too quick and too colloquial for them, though Raymond roared and laughed, while Sara, her specs firmly on her nose for once, watched with fascinated eyes a dear old woman, dressed in her best for the occasion even to a muff, hoping, as seemed likely, she would laugh herself right out of her seat and into the ring.

"Actually," Sara said reflectively, after about half an hour, leaning back with her eyes shut tight against the sight of some trapeze artistes, "I don't really like circuses at all—I hate performing animals, and I can't bear to watch tight-rope walkers and trapeze people because I always *know* they're going to fall."

"You will be glad you came then," Raymond murmured.

"But I *am*," Sara replied, opening her eyes for a second to remove the paper from a stick of nougat, and shutting them again, "that's the funny bit."

A burst of clapping announced the end of the trapeze act.

"Better look now, Sara," Caroline remarked. "Here's a friend of yours."

"Oh, who?" Sara bounced forward. "Oh, it's the ponies: look, there's Snowdrop, on the outside, next to us—*isn't* he a pet?" She kept up a running commentary of delight and praise, forgetting even to eat her nougat, as the four trotted round, in perfect precision, while a booted and spurred gentleman stood in the centre of the ring, twirling his mustachios and cracking a long whip, and a rather buxom equestrienne blew lavish kisses to the audience while nerving herself to take a running leap on to an unfortunate animal's back.

Once, twice they circled, changing obediently from a trot to a canter and back again at the word of command. The third time, as the ponies passed the Petit Chose trio, Snowdrop hesitated and turned his head towards them. As he reached the farthest side, something seemed to click in his brain. He stopped dead, turned, cantered across the ring and came to rest opposite Sara, his two forefeet up on the barrier, with as eager and expectant a look on his nice face as you could hope to see.

"The *darling*!" cried Sara, in an ecstasy: "he's smelled the nougat!"

The lady with the muff screamed, the booted and spurred gentleman cracked his whip and shouted orders, his moustachios bristling with fury, the stout lady stopped blowing kisses and stood staring, her mouth a little open, the other ponies, dull things these, trotted on, round and round. The rest of the audience, who in their simple way doubtless looked on it all as part of the performance, laughed and cheered.

Caroline who felt the whole great tent was full of eyes, nothing but eyes, all of them fixed on her, was red with embarrassment.

"Now you've done it, you silly fathead!" she

muttered, doing her best to look as if she had nothing to do with Sara, who, quite oblivious to the sensation, was murmuring endearments and stripping a fresh stick of nougat for the insatiable animal. Raymond, who never had any sense of responsibility, as Caroline told herself in a fury, was laughing loudest of all.

After what seemed a hundred years to Caroline, long training reasserted itself. A particularly loud scream from his master recalled Snowdrop to a sense of duty, and, after a last gentle snatch for a final tit-bit, he trotted off, contentedly munching, and went through the rest of his act without faltering; the whole troupe being rewarded at the end with loud and prolonged applause.

Caroline cautiously came out of her retirement —in the corner of her seat farthest from Sara— and hissed out of the side of her mouth:

"Stark, staring mad—you'll be the death of me. You shouldn't be allowed out."

"Calm yourself, my poor Caroline," Raymond soothed. "The good man will doubtless put the idea into his act and so make his fortune."

Better for Caroline's peace of mind if she had fulfilled her threat, now breathed again from the side of her mouth, and taken Sara home there and then: for worse was to come.

Item Ten, said the programme, Professor Gérard with his Wonder Chimpanzees, Lulu, Babette, and Susette. On he came, the noble Professor, leading Susette, in a little red skirt, by the hand, with Babette, in a little blue skirt, and Lulu, in natty yellow trousers and straw hat, ambling at his heels.

Susette was the baby of the act, and rather skittish. The other two rode their little bicycles or sat in their little chairs, reading their newspapers or taking a cup of coffee, very peacefully; Susette had to be coaxed before she would do her tricks, and occasionally would amuse herself by surreptitiously pinching Babette or snatching at Lulu's hat. Even that did not satisfy her, because something, perhaps the call of freedom, perhaps the desire for a hat of her own, unappeased by her attempts on Lulu's, must have been gnawing at Susette's vitals, for suddenly, when the Professor's eye was off her for a moment, she streaked across the ring, straight—of course—to where Sara was sitting, hopped over the barrier, grabbed Sara's beret, and was away up the aisle towards the exit, chattering happily.

Sara hadn't wanted to wear her beret, she didn't even treasure it very much, but she wasn't going to be done down by a monkey—and a French monkey at that. She let out a yell and gave chase.

The Professor, leaving Babette and Lulu to a hastily summoned assistant, wasn't far behind her; and a motley assortment of small boys formed a vociferous rear-guard.

The audience rose to their feet. Half of them had not the faintest idea of what had happened, but every one was ready with a theory when, inevitably, the bright thought struck some one—probably the lady with the muff:

"Fire, it's a fire! The monkey knew! Save yourselves!" and the stampede began. The ringmaster might shout himself hoarse, the band might heroically fiddle or valiantly trumpet in vain endeavour to stop the riot—the wise monkey knew, thought all, and there was certainly a fire. Shouting, jostling, pushing, the inhabitants of St. Brioc saved themselves. . . .

Caroline and Raymond, aghast, huddled in their seats in an empty tent.

"We'd better find her," said Caroline faintly at last, and they crept cautiously out, terrified lest they be recognised as associates of Sara's and denounced by the circus people as alarmists and wreckers of honest folks' livelihood. They wormed their way through the crowd, now standing outside quite happily, waiting to see the blaze and get their money's worth that way at least. By the time they had sidled as unobtrusively as possible to the back of the crowd the proprietor had come forth, and, with tears in his eyes, was assuring the audience that there was no fire, there never had been a fire, and, *le bon Dieu* and all the saints assisting, there never would be a fire. No tiniest danger would ever touch them within his circus tent. "*Entrez, alors!*" he wound up. "*Entrez, mesdames et messieurs.*"

Caroline and Raymond did not enter. They had spotted Sara. There she was, panting, red of face, hair wild, at the edge of the multitude, on tiptoe, stretching her little neck to its uttermost in an effort to see over the crowd, turning to right and left with eager, impatient questions.

Caroline and Raymond removed her.

"Oh, there you are, you two! I say, what's going on? What is it? Have I missed it?"

"On the contrary," Raymond replied "you did it."

Caroline looked at her almost in admiration: "It's amazing! She must only be semi-conscious. Starts a riot and asks what all the fuss is about! Take her home, Raymond: she's one too many for me."

"And *what have you done with the monkey?*" Raymond was fierce.

"What are you all talking about?" Sara was bewildered in her mind and uncomfortable in her body as they frog-marched her along the road. "You're crazy. I never touched the beastly monkey—I couldn't get within a mile of it. It made for the shore and went round the cliff towards the *grève* and I wasn't going after it in the dark. And I met the Prof. He called me a ' *jeune fille héroïque*.' " Caroline snorted. " Of course I didn't tell him I was after my beret all the time. He had to give up the chase too, naturally; and he was nearly in tears, poor man, for his poor Susette out alone in the dark. Now do hang off, you two—you'd think I was an escaped looney or something. And I wish you'd tell me what all the crowd were outside for. And what had I got to do with it?"

"Listen, Unconscious—and I'm serious. Have you never been taught to *control* yourself in a crowd? You needn't answer, I know you have. Three times a year to my own knowledge, every time we go to a concert in the town, in fact, we have a full-dress lecture from wee Froggie never to scream or make a fuss if there's any excitement or bother. And what do you do? Rush out of the tent yelling at the pitch of your voice——"

"I was after that monkey and I didn't——" Sara was beginning in an aggrieved tone, but Caroline was as steel.

"Shut up. The prisoner at the bar isn't allowed

to argue. Raymond, you stop cackling. Sara, do you realise that half those people had no idea the chimp had departed, with all sorts of turns going on at once? All they saw and heard was a female run screaming from the place, with a small crowd soon at her heels. Of course they thought it was a fire."

"Oh, gosh, they didn't? Did they stampede? Oh, gosh, how awful! Oh, Caro, I must go back— no, let go my arms—I must see if any one was hurt."

"No one was," said Raymond. "We should have heard about *that*."

Raymond's torch discovered Rest-and-be-thankful, and they paused there, looking back to St. Brioc. The tent was a patch of light, and, very faintly, they could hear the music of the band.

"It will go on now most of the night," said Raymond.

"*What* a pity you made us leave so early, Caro, and miss all the fun," sighed Sara, herself again.

CHAPTER IX

NEXT morning, Raymond mentioned that Papa and he were going back to Paris for a couple of days.

"Papa has some work to do, and I"—solemnly—"have a very important examination. We'll bring back the little auto when we come—it was being repaired."

"I do hope you pass your old exam.," said Sara. "I never do."

"Oh, but it's nothing. I shall do very well. Without doubt my papers will be so brilliant they will make me President of the Republic immediately."

"What happens if you fail?" Caroline wanted to know. Sara was thinking how nice it would be to know the President of the Republic, and considered Caroline's remark to be in the worst possible taste, so she hurriedly changed the subject.

"Well, if you're going to be packing and that, I vote we go down to St. Brioc and get some stamps and things. What do you think, Caroline?"

Caroline was doubtful about Sara's being seen
in St. Brioc at all, but as she was in rather a
chastened mood this morning she felt she could
probably manage her, so they set off.

For stamps they patronised a little shop—not
on the quay, but tucked away in a little cobbled
street which wandered up the hill to the rather
grander part of the village where some villas
overlooked the farther bay—for the simple
reason that on exploring the various shops they
had discovered in this one some rather battered
tins of McVitie and Price's biscuits displayed.
Caroline seemed to think this was a great tribute
to British enterprise, and though the biscuits,
when they had bought a few, proved that it
couldn't have been very recent enterprise, she
refused to take her custom elsewhere. Her
loyalty wasn't without its reward, for the shop
was owned by the two most delightful women,
fat as tubs, with round, rosy faces and little
twinkling boot-button eyes, and although their
hard, Breton speech was practically unintelligible
to the girls, they all got on very well, by signs
and pointing and a lot of giggling. They sold,
it seemed, everything in their little shop, and
besides stamps (which were kept loose, in a drawer,
beside the matches) the two to-day were collecting
an odd assortment of chocolate, a thriller (recom-

mended to Sara by Madame, as ardent a detective-fan as herself), a more sober volume in the Tauchnitz edition for Caroline, who thought it quite bad enough to speak French without reading it, some candles to replace those at home which somehow seemed to melt away very quickly —Caroline having vowed herself quite unable to meet Yvonne's reproachful glance at the sight of the guttered candles another morning. Post-cards, too, had to be chosen, with the assistance of one Madame, while the other Madame served a very small boy who clip-clopped in with his very large sabots.

Sara had put on her glasses, being certain that much more exciting stories were to be had from the topmost shelves, and was taking advantage of them to have a good look round when she suddenly clutched Caroline's arm.

"Sardines," she said.

Caroline shot a hurried glance at her. "It's happened at last," she said to herself: "she's gone off her rocker. I must be very patient with her."

"And cheese," said Sara, getting more excited and pointing, in spite of all her mother's teaching, at rows of little round boxes of *petit Gruyère*.

"Yes, yes, sardines and cheese. What about them, darling?" The unusual endearment would have caused Sara as much surprise as Caroline's bedside manner if she had not been too full of her big idea to notice either.

"Breakfast, of course. Don't be so *slow*, Caroline. Brighter Breakfasts! You're always going on about its being more *petit* than *déjeuner* and what wouldn't you give for a good plate of bacon and eggs. Well, we can't manage a fry, but I'm very fond of a nice sardine."

Caroline was thankful that Sara's symptoms were no worse than usual, after all, but she had to remonstrate, for form's sake if nothing else.

"Can't abide sardines, myself," she said.

"Well, but you can have cheese."

"What about Madame? She might be frightfully offended and I'd hate that. I mean, we get grand food, really—only it's different——"

"But Madame wouldn't *know*. We'd slink the empties out with our bathing things and bury them on the beach."

"Sardines are so messy——" Caroline was weakening. "Oh, all right then, don't look so miserable." So a tin of sardines and a box of cheese went into their bags, after a little incredulity on the part of the two Mesdames.

With a halt at Rest-and-be-thankful for the consumption of the usual bag of peaches the girls arrived back at Petit Chose in time to shake hands with the Duvals, who were all there, the young ones, come to say good-bye to their idolized Raymond.

"You'd think he was going to the North Pole at least," Caroline, who liked to retreat into the most distant corner of the *salon* when any Duvals were about, muttered. Sara was telling Régine, who really wasn't so bad, only rather like a cow, she thought, such extracts from the circus episode as she considered suitable. Ajax, that amiable fool of a dog, was being fussed over by Miette, whose admiration for Raymond transferred itself to his most remote belongings. Monique was kissing Madame, and Pierre was alternately squeaking and growling at Monsieur in the garden. Raymond himself was nowhere to be seen, but suddenly the door crashed open, and he was upon them. Literally, in the case of the ill-starred Ajax. If both had been stretched dead at their feet the Duvals could not have set up a greater lament. Raymond got up, and the sight of a thin trickle of blood from a scratch on his knee brought Régine and Monique to his side with cries of sympathy and horror. Miette, unable to get near him for her elder sisters, turned to Ajax with the misguided notion that he would like to be kissed at this point, and, to Caroline's intense and secret satisfaction, got well bitten for her pains. The row was enough to bring in Monsieur, who usually held aloof from such scenes, with a suggestion that Raymond, who hadn't opened his mouth, should not create such an uproar. Régine turned to tell him indignantly that blood—Raymond's blood—had been spilt, and the wounded one made his escape with a grin on his face to try the remedy of a little cold water. Miette attempted to raise a spot of sympathy on her own account, but without success, and peace was restored. Sara, for one, was delighted to see Louise come in then and hear her "Madame is served."

"Now if they hurry up and say good-bye we'll maybe get hot soup for once," she said to Caroline, who sniffed sceptically. Once the Duvals had been despatched and they had hurried in to lunch she was consoled, however, by the sight of her favourite dish at Petit Chose, a luscious concoction of liver and prunes, but one which Sara wasn't so keen on, because, she had averred on its last appearance, she never got anything but prunes. Caroline had been unmoved. "You should wear your specs," she had said. "And anyway, you shouldn't be so greedy."

After luncheon they waved good-bye to Monsieur and Raymond, as the wagonette trundled them away to the station.

"What about exploring the cave?" Caroline

I

said firmly as they turned back to the house. Sara looked slightly green, but Caroline went on ruthlessly. "We could bathe in that cove for a change, at the same time."

"Well, I might explore the cave," answered Sara courageously, at length. "But bathe in the Haunted Bay I won't. It would be sacrilege or something."

"Sacrilege, my foot! It's funk," said Caroline rudely. "Come on." They collected bathing things and some *goûter* from Marie la Cuisinière, and Caroline thought they had better take a candle as they hadn't a torch, and set off, Sara still protesting.

"No, honestly, Caroline, it doesn't seem the proper thing to me," she said, for about the twentieth time, when they had scrambled down the cliff side and stood surveying an innocent-looking little bay, not unlike their own *grève*, with its pebbly beach and occasional masses of rock. On their right loomed the cave with a small, low mouth which struck Sara as very sinister, but the water was calm and blue, the sun shone bravely and Sara began to feel a little bolder, but still adamant about bathing.

"All right, then, I'll go in by myself," and Caroline retired behind a rock to undress.

As she watched Caroline sporting in the sea, Sara talked to herself to keep her spirits up.

"It's all very well for Caroline to be so snotty about ghosts, but, gosh—look at my Great-Aunt Alison—she *lived* in a haunted house and she told me all about their nasty habits—specially the way hers always blew out her candle at night at a certain spot. . . . I should have *died* . . . still, I don't suppose old Philippe would show up during the day. . . . And it would be an experience to see him—maybe. . . . I've a jolly good mind to go and have a look while Caroline's in the sea. Thinks I'm a funk, does she? Well, I'll jolly well show her—I'll go by myself. Where's that candle? And matches. Oh, blow!—left my specs at home. . . . It's quite an ordinary-*looking* cave, really. . . . Gosh, I wonder if I hadn't better wait for Caro, after all? In case it's full of bandits or that . . . Oh, gosh, I'll have to go on, now! I *wish* I'd never thought of it." But it was too late, for her peace of mind, to draw back; she was at the very cave-mouth, her hand was fumbling with a match—at the third attempt she got the candle lit, but at the cost of the matches which dropped from her nerveless hands into a convenient little pool.

The entrance to the cave was narrow, and little light filtered into the farther corners; as Sara advanced cautiously and raised her candle she saw dank walls rising to a great height and disappearing into the darkness; to her right the feeble gleam of the candle failed to penetrate the shadows. She clung to the left hand-wall and advanced.

"Gosh, it's bigger than I thought it would be! Actually," she thought, "I can't see what happens over there. I'll just go on along this wall and I must come to the passage sometime. I'll go back when I find it—it really wouldn't be fair not to wait for Caroline."

The cave seemed to be still opening out, and after she had crept along a little way, it bent sharply to the left: no light from the entrance reached here, but the candle put up a brave show; and Sara determinedly ignored the depths of gloom its efforts did not illumine, and the fantastic, flickering shadows.

"Well, this isn't so bad. I didn't *think* Philippe would be about in the daytime." She began to feel almost jaunty, and her heart resumed a more normal beat. Suddenly, a drop of hot wax on her hand made her jump and look at the flame. It was being blown to one side.

"Must be some draughts about here. Maybe I'm near the passage and there's a crack somewhere. I *hope* it's a draught. I can't see any wall

on the other side. I can't see anything but
darkness. Oh, gosh, I——" she felt a rush of cold
air on her face—and the candle went out. Her
heart gave a sickening lurch, and she stopped
dead, frozen with terror. She remembered with
grief the matches in the pool outside. Desperately
she refused to let her mind dwell on ghosts—
ghosts who blew out candles!

"It's a draught, I know it's a draught. I must
get back. I must get back." She huddled against
the wall, the darkness close about her, listening
for she knew not what. Memories of a childhood
remedy against the horrors of the dark came to
her, and she hunted round her paralysed brain
for a hymn-tune. "Hark the herald angels
sing——" she quavered, inappropriately enough,
but the sound of her own voice, high, unnatural
in that confined and echoing space, terrified her
more than the silence and the carol came to an
abrupt and squeaky end. She turned round,
pushed the useless candle into her pocket, kept
her right hand on the wall and tottered forward,
her left hand outstretched. She stumbled on for
a few steps and stopped again. What was that?
There was a sound. A soft, indefinite, slurring
sound. Of faint shuffling, ghostly feet? Sara kept
swallowing her heart, which had in some peculiar
way jumped right up to the back of her throat.

She took a step forward, and her hand, instead of empty air, met something soft, and warm, and *hairy*. Her last poor remnants of courage left her. She let out a yell, and, heedless where she might go, dashed forward as quickly as her shaking legs would carry her, scraping her hand along the wall to guide her, slipping and tripping over the uneven ground, panic-stricken. . . .

Caroline, sunning herself after her bathe and wondering where the precious ass Sara had got to, turned to see the most amazing sight—the precious ass, her eyes starting out of her head, screaming, "Help, Caroline! Save me, save me!" shooting out of the cave as if fiends were at her heels, and stumbling over the shore. And behind her lumbered poor Susette, wakened out of a sleep on the cold hard ground, so unlike her usual soft bed, heartily sick of freedom, and delighted with a sight of one of those nice humans who suggested some hope of seeing again her dear Professor and a good dinner.

Sara flung herself on Caroline, half-sobbing, burying her face. "It's Philippe. It's the ghost. I *touched* him, Caro. I touched his horrible beard—it was warm, and *hairy*. Don't dare laugh, I touched him!"

"Sara, you lunatic, get up. It was only——" Something indeed made Sara look up, and, as if she hadn't had enough to endure, she screamed again as she saw the new terror, a wild beast which seemed to have appeared from nowhere, fling a hateful long arm round Caroline's neck.

"Caro! Look out! It'll strangle you." But Caroline was laughing and patting Susette and trying to disengage that affectionate arm and to assure Sara that destruction, neither from ghosts nor savage animals, was imminent. And when at last Sara understood, she rolled over on her back and gasped and choked with the laughter of pure relief until Caroline had visions of having to treat her for hysterics as well as all her other troubles.

"We'll have some tea, and then we'll all feel better," she said firmly, slapping Susette's fingers. For Susette had had the same idea long ago and was already poking into the tea-basket.

The girls had the tea and Susette had the bread and butter and chocolate.

"We've had many a queer meal in France, but this is the queerest yet," said Caroline, smiling fondly on their guest who was really behaving beautifully. Sara, quite her old self again, went on and on about her dreadful experiences in the cave and Caroline admitted that it must have been pretty grim when the candle went out. "And there must have been a good current of air from somewhere to do it," she said. "Your lovely rendering of a Christmas Carol—what on earth made you pick on that?—must have disturbed Susette who was probably a bit fed-up and lonely. I wonder what she thought of you as a singer."

"She thought I was a lovely singer—didn't you, darling?"

"She must have wandered along the shore last night and gone into the cave. We could leave all our stuff here and take her round to St. Brioc by the shore—if she'll come."

Susette came all right, between the two of them, amiably giving each a paw. They negotiated the rocks and sea-weed safely, and caused no small sensation when they reached such civilisation as St. Brioc provided. People on the beach stared and pointed and exclaimed, children stopped their games and followed, and they reached the circus at the head of quite a little procession, Caroline red and miserable, Sara thoroughly enjoying herself again and explaining, to all who asked, how they had found the chimpanzee along the shore and were now about to return her to her owner.

Him they found, hot and distressed, after a fruitless morning's search, having an altercation with the local *gendarme* who admitted himself ready and willing to cope with a lost watch, or a

lost child, but hopelessly unable to cope with a
lost chimpanzee. Other members of the circus
were gathered round, offering comments and
advice.

When he saw the procession coming towards
him, his little Susette between the two girls,
Professor Gérard rushed towards them, and—an
emotional man—clasped Sara in his arms and
kissed her, first on the right cheek, then on the
left; next, to Caroline's horror, he treated her in
like manner; Susette then was seized and alternately petted and scolded. When he showed signs
of going through the whole performance again
Caroline nudged Sara violently and mumbled:

"Better clear out of here."

Sara, and the crowd, thought all this was the
best entertainment they had had for a while, but
she knew Caroline's views on scenes and publicity
generally so she told the Professor earnestly that
it had been a pleasure to bring Susette back, and
no, truly, they didn't want half of all he pos-
sessed as a reward, nor, although it was very kind
of him, did they want free seats for the circus that
night. And hadn't Susette better have something
to eat, because she seemed pretty hungry? This
was a master-stroke; the Professor, striking his
clenched fist against his forehead at his stupidity,
thanked them again a million times, wrung them

by the hand and finally led Susette off to have some dinner, leaving the girls free to depart, Sara bowing to the admiring throng.

"There's still time to explore the cave before dinner," said Caroline, as they clambered back round the foot of the cliffs.

But she got no answer, for Sara had swooned.

CHAPTER X

BRIGHTER BREAKFASTS

SARA lay in bed next morning, the warm sun on her, wondering why she had a pleased, rather excited feeling. She always had that, in the morning, in France, but to-day there was something definite. Suddenly it came to her— sardines! She had a slight qualm as she prodded her little tummy under the bed-clothes. "I have to let the belt on my shorts out three more holes these days, but it's all gorgeous food." She lay in a happy daze, thinking of the potatoes, in slices, dripping with melted butter, that fish affair they had on Fridays sometimes, with the exquisite unusual flavour which Caroline said was cheese but which was like no cheese Sara had ever tasted before. Or chicken, with pale yellow sauce all over it. Or that pie which when opened revealed, most surprisingly, sweet-breads. Or the *crêpes*, brown and crinkly, with eggs inside. Or, most luscious of all, the chocolate pudding, thin and smooth as velvet, which Madame maintained was not nearly as good as the one her Paris cook made, Marie la Cuisinière being but a local person and quite without subtlety in the culinary arts.

Sara always opened wide eyes at this view, and made a vow to herself that Madame must be visited in Paris.

"What are you thinking about, lying there with a soft grin on your face?" Caroline's sleepy early-morning voice demanded.

"Food," breathed Sara rapturously, coming to. "Oh, good, here's Louise!"

"*Bonjour, Mesdemoiselles. Il fait beau temps.*"

"*Bonjour*, Louise. Lovely weather, lovely breakfast. Lovely *sardines*," Sara shot at Caroline, as Louise set down the tray and left them to it.

"Lumme, I'd forgotten about those! I can't eat the things at the best of times and I certainly don't feel much like a sardine this morning."

"Well, actually, you don't look much like one," said Sara, thinking this was an awfully good joke, as she hopped out of bed and fished the tin of sardines and the cheese from her handkerchief drawer. "Here, how do you open these beastly things? There's a sort of key-affair——"

"The great thing is," said Caroline sitting up, "to get the key the right way round, otherwise it gets stuck when the tin's half-open and you can't turn it. Better give it to me."

"No, look, I'll be terribly careful. That's right, I'm sure. It's opening beautifully—oh, blow! It's stuck!"

"Well done, fathead. Now what?"

"I'll have to poke them out. Gosh, the spoons are too small. I know—a toothbrush." Sara collected a toothbrush, and, jumping back into bed, proceeded to coax the sardines out of their box with it. Caroline whose initial dislike of the fish was not improved by the sight of the mangled oily bodies which the toothbrush—hers at that— was bringing forth, gloomily watched large drops of oil falling on to Sara's sheets and counter-pane.

"A fine mess you're making," she said, helping herself to cheese. "This room'll smell of sardines for days." Sara said nothing but grinned blissfully, her mouth full of sardine. "And for goodness' sake," Caroline went on, "keep that tin out of Madame's sight. . . ."

As she might have known, her warning was wasted, for, about an hour later, as they, ready for the *grève*, took leave of Madame in the *salon*, Sara, with a muttered "Did I remember to put in my bathing-cap?" quite thoughtlessly emptied her beach-bag and there on the floor, right in front of Madame's astonished eyes, dropped the sardine-tin.

"Ah?" said Madame.

"Oh!" said Caroline, getting pink.

"Oh, that!" said Sara, picking it up nonchalantly. She turned earnestly to Madame, "It's Caroline's. Yes," she hurried on before the feelings of the other two expressed in Madame's raised eyebrows and Caroline's face of fury, should find words, "yes, it's a queer thing, but every now and then Caroline has a sudden passion for sardines—eats tins of them at a time. We didn't want to bother you, of course. It's in the family, as a matter of fact, her grandfather was just the same."

Madame was most interested, although the corner of her mouth twitched.

"But you should have told me, my little one. How long do those attacks last?" She addressed Caroline but it was Sara who, warming to her theme, replied:

"Oh, a day or two, sometimes not so long: it depends how many she can get a hold of. She goes all queer if she doesn't get them—foams at the mouth, and that."

Caroline, looking as if she would foam at the mouth at any moment, nodded dumbly as Madame turned to her for confirmation of these assertions.

"We must see what we can do, Caroline," said Madame kindly. "I would not like to see you suffer. And now you are going off to bathe? The tide will not be in yet, so wait for me—I shall join you in perhaps an hour, and we can

bathe all together. Ah, no, leave the box, Sara—
Louise will remove it. *A bientôt*."

"*A bientôt*, Madame." Sara showed an inclination to linger and chat, but Caroline gathered up
the bathing things and hurried her off.

"You blithering ass!" said Caroline, as soon as
they were out of earshot. "What did you want to
go and say a fool thing like that for? Foam at
the mouth if I don't get sardines——"

"Well, but darling, it was the only single thing
I could think of as an excuse. Wasn't it an
agonizing moment? Gosh, I think I was jolly
quick-witted, on the whole. Kind of like Napoleon,
or somebody——"

"*Kind* of. Why not *you* foam at the mouth?"
Caroline was not to be side-tracked. "You
don't imagine for one moment that Madame
believed you, do you?"

"Gosh, Caroline, I did my best—a girl can't
do more, can she?"

"Your best will have us all in an asylum or a
prison, one of these days." But she was grinning
now, and when Sara saw that she gave a great
whoop and careered round the last few bends of
the steep path shouting, "*Vive* Caroline! *Vive*
the sardine-fiend!" with Caroline, stopping to
pick up the odds and ends of towels and caps she
shed as she ran, not long behind her. . . .

"Hope the Duvals don't turn up this morning," said Caroline, as they lay on a rock, sun-bathing. "Sara, I've been thinking we ought to ask them to tea one day. They did have us after all, and we're going to dinner there next Saturday, when Raymond comes back."

"What? Ask them to Petit Chose? But they've been there to tea. Don't tell me you've forgotten—and we didn't get a bite to eat even although they brought their own eats as well and had them in our dining-room!"

"'Course, I haven't forgotten. I never saw anything so peculiar in my life."

"I couldn't make it out at all, and I didn't like to ask Raymond whether Madame had just asked them on the spur of the moment at the *grève* and they brought their picnic along, or whether it's a French custom to bring your own food when you go out to tea. They're so odd about tea altogether. I wonder——"

"I meant, to have tea at St. Brioc, in the sumptuous Hôtel de le Plage," Caroline interrupted, ignoring Sara's irrelevancies and going back to the point under discussion, "or that 'English Tea-shop' everybody tells us about so proudly, but which we've never found. I don't expect they have much fun really, and they have been rather decent to us even if they are so wet."

"Gosh, d'you think it'll be fun having tea with us? I hate them like poison——"

"All right, we won't then. Although you don't really. Hate them, I mean."

"Of course I don't. And it's a beautiful idea, Caro, darling, because if we return hospitality or whatever you call it, then we needn't be polite to them any more, need we? The way you're always insisting because we've eaten their salt."

"We'll ask Madame. And I vote we have them to-day——"

"Yes, when Raymond's away. They'll be *furious*."

"No, because the tide's out now in the afternoon and we haven't got four for tennis, and it won't spoil another afternoon when there are lots of things doing. There's Madame, coming down the path. Now we can bathe. . . ."

Caroline had entirely forgotten the sardine episode by lunch-time, but it was brought back in full force when, before she had finished her soup, Louise brought in and laid before her a plate piled high with—sardines. Her eyes glazed with horror, she stared at their nauseating oiliness; she glanced at Madame, who was smiling as if glad to have pleased Caroline, and at Sara, grinning with unholy glee.

"How *kind* of you, Madame!" said Sara. "Isn't it kind of Madame, Caroline?"

"Very kind," Caroline answered, and picked up a fork. "I'll show the little beast," she thought. "I can imagine the row she'd have kicked up if she'd had a plate of onions or something she hated put down before her." With a slight air of an Early Christian martyr going to the stake she finished them, to the last tail—much to Sara's annoyance, who was longing to hear Caroline's stumbling excuses—but at the cost of refusing some succulent looking veal and compôte of fruit, which distressed Madame.

"Is the attack over, Caroline, or will you have more sardines at dinner?" she asked, and Caroline, blushing slightly as she looked at Madame's mocking face, said thankfully, "I don't want to see another sardine for years, if not for ever, thank you, Madame. And it'll teach me," she thought savagely, "*never* to give in to that idiot's daft schemes. Her and her Brighter Breakfasts."

Actually, it was Caroline who did have the last laugh, for after a little conversation with Madame that evening, a fried egg, in the neatest little flat dish just big enough to hold it, appeared next morning and every subsequent morning. "For Mademoiselle Caroline," said Yvonne.

"Well, of all the rotten favouritism!" Sara mourned.

Caroline looked up from her egg innocently.

"But Sara, I thought you liked the French breakfast? I told Madame you did," she said.

CHAPTER XI

THE GREAT WATCH RACKET

MADAME had agreed to the Duval party, but declined the invitation to join them, having to go and visit the sick wife of a farmer on one of her farms nearby. Mme. Duval, too, thought it was charming of the girls, and despatched her offspring with her blessing, all but poor Pierre whom she kept at home in spite of his wordy remonstrances.

Sara and Caroline felt really rather important at the thought of giving a real party in a real hotel. The hotel to be sure was not very imposing and, as far as they had ever been able to discover, wasn't capable of housing more than a dozen visitors at a time; but the waiter, a most fatherly person, ushered Caroline, who insisted on being in command as being less of a menace than Sara, on to a balcony overlooking the sands and most pleasantly screened by hydrangeas, a mass of faint mauve flowers. Her approval having been graciously given, he drew up an iron table and little iron chairs and they all sat down. The idea of tea proper never entered the Duvals' heads:

they chose Grenadine syrup to a man. Sara had
citronnade—she loved the way it was served to her
in Brittany—all raw, sugar and water and a
lemon, a lemon-squeezer and an empty glass on a
little white saucer with the price marked on it in
blue letters. It kept her happy for hours, making
her own drink, and the fact that she never got it
quite right, but always too sweet or too sour,
never took away from her pleasure. Caroline had
tea, with the usual little basket to catch the leaves
hanging from the teapot's nose and hot milk.
The waiter growing more paternal every minute,
brought the best the hotel had to offer—two
large baskets of bread, a plate of *brioches*, a plate
of wafer biscuits, butter and a dish of jam—and
beamed at them all. Yes, the Duvals thought
they would like something more to drink now—
limonade this time; Sara, thinking the table
looked a little bare, produced two half-pound
blocks of chocolate she had bought in the village;
very soon Caroline had to call for more bread,
more *brioches*, and more lemonade until Sara,
hopelessly outclassed at her own game, sat back
and watched their guests, fascinated.

"Gosh, they can't have seen food for a week,"
she managed to mutter, in English, under cover
of the general noise and bonhomie.

"Shut up, they'll hear you."

When the ninth empty lemonade bottle was ranged on the table with its fellows, and the last crumb of chocolate was disappearing down Monique's throat, Sara spoke again, anxiously, through shut teeth: "Got enough money?"

"'Mm. Just, I should think."

The Duvals leaned back in their little iron chairs and smiled. In the silence of repletion Sara thought she might take a photograph and said so, and had the three Duvals all keyed up to it, and getting their brightest smiles ready before she realised she had left her camera at home.

"It does not matter," said Miette, bearing her disappointment well. "We have at least had a delightful *goûter*."

"We had heard of your English tea," said Régine. "And to think that you have a repast like that every afternoon in your country! What pleasure, and what a country! My sisters, we shall drink a toast to England and our kind hostesses!" It meant two more bottles of lemonade, but Caroline and Sara appreciated the compliment all the same.

"What do *we* do?" said Caroline, as their guests toasted "*Angleterre!*" "Sing the Marseillaise?"

"Gosh, that's an idea! They'd like that." Sara, in her enthusiasm, so often mistook Caroline's brand of humour. Fortunately Caroline was spared the embarrassment for the Duvals liked this toasting enormously; nothing could stop them: they toasted Caroline and Sara next, then Madame, then Raymond and Monsieur and good luck to Raymond's exam., then Maman and the absent Pierre, then Sara and Caroline again. But a move towards a fourteenth bottle for the toasting of Ajax struck Caroline as excessive, so she forgot her no-French rule for once and broke up the party with a laconic but final speech of thanks.

"Though what I was thanking them for, I'd like to know?" she demanded of Sara, when they had deposited the Duvals at their own house and were having a much-needed rest on their backs at the side of a cornfield, gazing up at the blue of sky above them and the scarlet of poppies nodding by their side.

"Well, you find that in France," Sara theorized. "You go about all day being flowery and making great polite speeches—no sense at all if you stopped to think, but you never get time. Personally, I like it."

"Well, I think it's daft." Caroline rose, rather languidly. "Let's go home and I'll challenge you to a game of tennis. Wonder what the time is?"

"Caroline! Oh, gosh!" Sara cried, and Caroline, glancing down, saw her looking at her bare wrist in anguish. "I've lost my watch! Oh, what'll I do? We simply must go back to the hotel—I must have lost it at tea because I remember looking at it then. Oh, dear! Caro, come on. Or on the path, it might be, we'll have to search every *inch*. And maybe those beastly goats have eaten it by now." As she gabbled she was searching round where they had been lying, her specs well forward on her nose, while Caroline leaned up against the gate and regarded her lazily.

"Can't think what you're making such a fuss about. If it'll ease your mind any, and make you dry up I'll willingly *give* you five bob to get another in the first Marks and Spencer's we see when we get home."

"But that's just the point," Sara wailed. "It isn't my Marks and Spencer—it's my good one that Mummy said I wasn't to bring. But I loved it so much I couldn't bear to be parted from it. I didn't mean to wear it, but I did to-day, seeing it was a party. And I *loved* it, and there'll be a simply frightful row too, because there was a bit of a row when I went in bathing with my last one, do you remember? And Daddy vowed I wasn't ever going to have another until I could be more careful—and I am terribly careful only I seem to be unlucky, and then when he gave me this one for my birthday I was so thrilled—and what am I going to do?" Sara sat back on her heels and looked up at Caroline very pathetically.

"Oh, cheer up, Shrimp, it'll turn up all right. I didn't know you had brought it. We'll go back to the hotel now, and we can look along the path on the way down."

"Probably one of those blinking Duvals put her great hoof on it and crushed it to atoms—my *darling* watch."

If the cliff path were hiding Sara's watch it yielded not its secret; nor was the waiter any help. He was desolated, but alas, he was watchless.

"What *shall* I do now?" Sara demanded, a sick, helpless feeling at the pit of her stomach. Caroline, feeling for her, knowing how she had felt when her father gave her the watch, and how she doted on it, was determinedly brisk.

"We'll go to the police-station, if they have one in this place. Every other person seems to walk round in a uniform—some of them must be policemen."

"They've one *gendarme* at least," Sara was brightening a little, "because we saw him with the Prof., don't you remember?"

"'Mm, of course. Come to think of it, I wasn't so struck with his ability over that business," said

Caroline, who admired competence above all
things, as they hurried along the *plage* towards the
quay and the centre of the little town's activities.
"I vote we go straight to the mayor and get him
to put up a notice at the door of the town-hall
where the others are."

They were lucky enough to find M. le Maire
standing outside the Hôtel de Ville and talking
to, or rather bawling at, of all people, the self-
same *gendarme*. He, M. le Maire, was a fat little
man, so like the comic Frenchman of stage and
cartoon, with his tiny, well-trimmed black beard,
beady eyes, waisted coat and pointed shoes, that
Caroline, sturdy Briton, lost confidence in him at
once. He was giving the *gendarme* an awful time.

"This town," he was shouting, waving his
arms, "it is the home of vice, a sink of iniquity,
nursery of thieves and cut-throats——" Caroline
looked slightly incredulous at this, for a more
innocent, peaceful and peace-loving little town
than St. Brioc, she was certain, could not be
found. Sara's long face became even longer.
"You will bring the boy to me, Hercule—infamous
limb of Satan that he is to steal six apples from
the good Madame Dupont. I will make an
example of him that will terrify the evil-doers of
St. Brioc," he finished, dancing with excitement
and his arms working more like windmills than

ever. Caroline was somewhat nervous as to the effect on his already high blood-pressure of their news, but feeling that as Sara's watch had been lost, and not stolen, all might be well, she nudged Sara to get on with her little piece. She had reckoned without M. le Maire's preoccupation with the wrong-doing of the arch-criminal Josèphe-Marie, aged ten.

"A-a-ah! I knew it!" he announced triumphantly. "The fruit was but the first step. A watch, you say? He has stolen a watch, a valuable, beautiful watch. Yes, yes, yes, yes, Mademoiselle, I understand perfectly: but courage! It shall be returned if we have to turn him upside down and shake it out of him."

Sara, in her turn, tried to shout him down and to explain the real state of affairs, with no avail, for Josèphe-Marie had had occasion to borrow one or two of M. le Maire's prize peaches the previous Saturday, a thing not easily to be forgotten by that ardent peach-grower, although he was as a rule one of the most kindly of men.

What with M. le Maire and Sara shouting away at each other—at cross purposes and getting crosser, and with Hercule putting in an odd plea for young Josèphe-Marie, to whom he was devoted, Caroline felt the situation ought to be taken in hand. She pushed Sara aside, silenced the *gendarme's* obligato of sympathy with an imperious hand, fixed M. le Maire firmly with her eye and said, in her drawling, reluctant French, " Listen: Mademoiselle has lost—*lost* her watch, either near the Hôtel de la Plage or on the path leading up to Petit Chose, and we should be very grateful if you would put up a notice to that effect."

"Ah! Is that it? Why did Mademoiselle your friend tell me it had been stolen by Josèphe-Marie?" Caroline at this point held back the irate Sara from violence. "But naturally I shall be enchanted to affix a little notice—just there, where every one can see it. Enter, enter, and we shall compose it together."

He bustled them into a little ante-room, as spick and span as himself, and sat down at a desk laden with the most important looking documents.

"Always there is Government business," he said with a small shrug, carelessly slapping a pile of official papers with the air that it would go ill with the Government of France if M. le Maire of St. Brioc were not there to keep an eye on things, but that at the moment, for his part, he had something more pressing to attend to. "Well, then, what shall we say?" he asked, lifting a pen.

"I simply must get it back," said Sara, "because I'm very fond of my little watch; so we'd better offer a big reward—about a thousand francs, I should say——" M. le Maire nearly jumped out of his seat, Hercule looked very impressed, and Caroline said coldly:

"Have you got a thousand francs?"

"No, of course I haven't!" Sara hated to be bothered with niggling details when she had a big scheme on hand. "Daddy'll send it on, or you could lend it me—you've always got piles of money——"

"Better say five francs, Monsieur, if you please," Caroline interrupted.

"No, no, we must make it seem attractive," said Sara. "Could you say ' enormous reward '?— that'll fetch 'em."

"Five francs would be enormous to an inhabitant of our little town," said M. le Maire suddenly looking as if all the poverty of the ages was being borne by himself and St. Brioc, but he immediately perked up as he wrote out, "LOST! ENORMOUS REWARD!" in great big letters. "You are staying with Madame de St. Brioc, of course. The lucky one can bring his find to you there. . . ."

"That's about all we can do if we're not going to be terribly late for dinner," said Caroline, after they had watched M. le Maire pin up the notice in a most prominent position alongside the one which said, *Fête des Baigneurs: Bal de Nuit,* shaken hands for a long time with him and Hercule, and been bowed off the premises by both. Out of the tail of her eye Caroline saw Hercule hurrying off to rouse the village and start the search, so she assured Sara that all would be well. "All the same, that ' enormous reward ' business is the height of nonsense, although it would do you good to fork out a hundred francs or so."

"I'd willingly pay all I've got, Caro," said poor Sara, peering right and left on the ground as they toiled up the path once more.

"It's your willingness to pay all *I've* got that I'm not so keen on," said Caroline.

They were late, but Madame had been detained also, and she was too much distressed to hear of Sara's loss to bother about a spoiled meal.

"But it will be found, my little cabbage, have no fear," she said as they sat down to dinner. "And meantime you must forget all about it.

"When Armand brings the auto we must go some little excursions." If Madame were planning a hundred mile drive or a visit to St. Brieuc she always called it "a little excursion." "There are so many places, but the most interesting in the world is the Côtes-du-Nord or in Finistere. For example, quite often I take friends to see Kermaria-an-Isquit which is not far——"

"Oh, what's that, Madame?" Sara's spirits began to rise.

"It is a thirteenth-century chapel——" Sara's spirits fell again. "The name means ' the House of Mary the Health-Giver,' in Breton—is it not charming? There is a grim old wall-painting inside of the Dance of Death, and very old wooden statues of some of our Breton saints. They are enchanting, so crude and yet so smiling and kindly." Antiquities, unless they introduced blood-and-thunder, ghosts or treasure, hadn't much interest for Sara, but Caroline, who had a mild passion for history, old things and the lives of people who lived long ago, rather surprising in her outwardly matter-of-fact nature, was listening. Madame went on, feeling rather like a guide-book but determined not to let Sara brood on her loss. "It is beyond St. Quay, not far from Plouha—and that place should interest you, for after your English Charles I was defeated at—Naseby? Yes?—many of his followers crossed *La Manche* and took refuge there. Or we go sometimes to the Ile de Bréhat, a most lovely little island of pink rock off Paimpol——"

"An island?" queried Caroline. "I wouldn't like that at all."

Madame laughed. "Ah no, not the sea for

Caroline. Well, then, Paimpol is interesting—you have read Loti's *Pêcheur d'Islande*?"

"No, but every shop in St. Brioc except the fruiterer keeps trying to sell it to us," said Sara.

"I shall lend it to you, Sara."

Sara smiled her thanks and changed the subject: "Where else?"

"Oh, everywhere—Pointe du Raz, but that is rather far, perhaps, for the little auto, or Morlaix——"

"Morlaix!" broke in Caroline. "Sara, that's where our fathers stayed when they were kids."

"Gosh, I thought Morlaix was in the South of France." Sara was amazed.

"But the one place it is absolutely essential that you should see is the Mont St. Michel," Madame continued.

"I've heard of that. Like St. Michael's Mount in Cornwall, I suppose?"

"Like what? How d'you know all these things, Caroline? Tell us about it, Madame."

"You shall see it for yourself, Sara, I promise you—a great rock rising out of the sea with an ancient abbey on its summit, and little houses and shops on its slopes."

"Oh, if there are shops I'll like it." Sara was definite on that point. As they rose from table, Louise, whose face had been growing grimmer and grimmer with suppressed disapproval as she came and went from the kitchen serving dinner, addressed Madame:

"The kitchen, Madame, is full of peasants." Her voice was charged with a Parisian's disgust at these uncivilised Bretons. "And they all say they have found Mademoiselle Sara's watch."

Sara gave a little jump and a squeak of joy; Caroline and Madame looked at each other in consternation.

"I knew that enormous reward would do the trick," said Sara jubilantly, itching to be off to claim her lost property.

"Yes, but what trick?" Caroline asked dolefully.

Madame led them to the kitchen, Louise following in their wake, muttering. Indeed, the big, stone-flagged kitchen, its pots and pans gleaming in the light of the fire, seemed to be full to bursting of dark, smiling faces, but after the first shock Caroline counted six small boys, two young fishermen in their blue jerseys, and one ancient crone who leaned on a stick and who could only have reached Petit Chose at all by a miracle or a lift from M. le Boulanger. They gave Madame a great welcome, and the ubiquitous Josèphe-Marie, in his sabots and black pinafore, who was apparently first in the field, was pushed forward and exhorted to produce his exhibit. Which he did with pride and confidence. There was a deathly silence. It was a watch, all right, there was no mistaking that, but there the resemblance to Sara's ended. Impossible to know from whence Josèphe-Marie had unearthed that venerable turnip, but it had served its day and generation and should have been left to moulder in peace. Its face was begrimed out of all recognition, its case, once perhaps silver, was black where it wasn't green and carried many an honourable scar.

Sara gazed at it with wide eyes and listened spell-bound while Josèphe-Marie described with a wealth of detail just where on the path he had found it. Sara shook her head dumbly, and again even more dumbly when he asked in a tone of the greatest surprise if she were quite sure it wasn't her watch. That, and a word from Madame, made Josèphe-Marie retire, obviously astounded at his failure, and one by one the others were produced. Never can there have been such a collection of watches—they were all sizes, in varying stages of decay, two only were wrist-watches, one of them of gunmetal and brand-new, no doubt straight out of M. l'Horloger the watch-maker's; one had an Albert chain attached.

"I'm waiting for the crone to produce an hour-glass," giggled Caroline in Sara's ear. They were all laughing by this time: Madame gave the watch-finders a little mock lecture on greed which went in one ear and out the other, and instructed Marie le Cuisinière to give them cider and biscuits, which had a more permanent effect. What had almost developed into a party broke up then, and the small boys, the fishermen, and the crone took their departure, well enough pleased. It hadn't quite come off, they admitted to themselves philosophically, but it had been worth trying.

Ten more watches were offered to Sara during the evening, until the two of them were in a hysterical state, with Madame not much better, and greeting each announcement of a new claimant, come to say he had found Mademoiselle Sara's watch, with gales of laughter only to be stifled with much pain when actually in the presence of the villagers. Not that they minded a laugh or two; if there were any going that proved uncontrollable they joined in with a will.

"Sara, I can't bear much more," said Caroline at last. "I'm *aching* and I'm limp."

"You must have seen every watch in St. Brioc by this time," said Madame.

"I'm beginning to think it was almost worth losing it," said Sara. "I shall *never* forget your face, Caro, when that one, the butcher's son, produced that effort with no hands out of his beret, like a conjurer——"

"Well, I was all keyed up for a couple of white rabbits to come out next. Or the girl—who *was* it, Madame?—who said she hadn't actually found the watch, alas, but that her grandmother had second sight and would that help!" And they went off into the giggles again—Sara making the weirdest snorts and grunts, Caroline quite silent, only heaving slightly and with, as she would have told any one, the most awful pain—until Madame, not knowing the capacity of those two when they really got started on a bout of laughing, feared they would do themselves an injury.

"And now," she said, "now you must go to bed. When Armand and Raymond come back to-morrow we shall have a really careful search. And no more laughing! Good-night, my little ones, sleep well."

"Good-night, Madame." And they rollicked upstairs, Sara recalling some of the choicer incidents and setting Caroline going again at every other step, until they reached their room at last.

Sara pulled her sweater over her head and nearly finished, once and for all, the career of her ill-used glasses.

"Gosh, I must have had 'em on all day. That's

a record, Caroline. I put them on at the party to see Régine stuffing. Where's my spec-case— I'd better put them away. Gosh, Caroline, this *has* been a day—*gosh! Caro!*——"

Caroline, her mouth full of tooth-paste, turned to see Sara, no further on with her undressing, staring down at her open spectacle-case much as stout Cortez—whom she rather resembled by now—must have gazed at the Pacific.

"Don't tell me," spluttered Caroline, getting rid of the tooth-paste, "don't tell me. Let me guess. You've come to say you have found Mademoiselle Sara's watch."

CHAPTER XII

THEY MEET A MAN OF MYSTERY

"AND it was in your spectacle-case all the time, Sara?" Madame said next morning, overjoyed that the watch had been found, but more astonished than ever at the queerness of the English.

"Yes," Sara admitted shamefacedly and then hurried on, "you see, I quite often push things in it, for safety, money and that, and I remember now noticing at tea that the catch on my watch wasn't catching too well, so I put it in there in case—in case I *lost* it, and then forgot it, and I had my specs on all the time, and so I never looked in it again."

"Maybe it'll be a lesson to you," said Caroline, without much hope, gathering up the things to depart for the *grève*, followed by Madame and Sara still explaining how it all happened and how it wasn't so daft as it seemed.

They didn't wander far from the house that day, always expecting Papa and Raymond to arrive in the little auto, but it was dinner-time before they did. Raymond was cheerful, but obstinately silent as to the examination.

"I shall know in a fortnight," was all he would say. Madame sighed and changed the subject.

"If it's fine to-morrow," she said, "we shall go a little excursion to the Mont St. Michel. . . ."

When Sara wakened next morning something was sadly wrong. For the first time there was no sun. Annoyed, she shook her fist at the grey skies and prodded Caroline awake.

"Caroline," she mourned, "it's *dull* and maybe we won't be going to the Mont St. Michel."

"Who cares?" grunted Caroline. "Let a girl sleep, can't you?"

But she was as disappointed as Sara when Madame decided that it would be better to wait for a sunny day.

"I do not think it will rain, yet," she said. "But I want you to see the Mont when the sun is shining. Amuse yourselves at home to-day."

Raymond thought he would find Maturin *père* and go out with him in his boat: Caroline felt ill at the very thought, and Sara refused to go without her.

"We could go down to St. Brioc though, and buy things," she suggested eagerly, and so it was decided.

They went first to the embroidery shop and bought Breton lace mats and handkerchiefs for their mothers, and a wee one for Madame; then they went to the bric-a-brac shop and had a lovely time. Caroline bought a carved wooden head of an old peasant woman with a wrinkled face, which Sara thought quite hideous, for her father, and a comic little wooden man whose jaws cracked nuts for Vanessa. Sara, after much indecision and heart-burning, chose a card box for *her* father, who never by any chance played cards; corks with funny men's heads on top and paper-knives for the boys; an ash-tray because she liked it; and a huge doll, of no conceivable use either to herself or to any of her relatives, with long legs, beautifully dressed in peasant costume—"exact in every detail" the shop-woman assured her—because she fell in love with it, and christened it Marie Thérèse on the spot.

"Though how you're going to get it home, I don't know," Caroline, who considered Sara's sudden fancies to be signs of a deranged mind, reminded her. The shop-woman did her best. She packed it lovingly into a huge box—"like a coffin," Sara giggled—and they set off home bearing it between them, their other parcels festooned round.

"If Hercule saw us he'd think we had bumped some one off and were carrying home the body," Sara said.

"I wish you'd keep the body still: you will keep skipping about and bumping it against my shins."

"Well, gosh, you've got such long legs, I've got to trot to keep up with you."

Caroline grinned and said sorry and slowed down, and Sara added, "Now I come to think of it, we'd better go and tell M. le Maire we found my watch, hadn't we?"

"Not unless you have a great passion to see him," Caroline replied, "for Madame sent word down yesterday—otherwise we should still have been interviewing maniacs with grandfather clocks, I dare say."

"Oh, that's all right then. It's amazing how people seem to do things before I get time to. It's not that I haven't the best intentions, but something always seems to go wrong with them half-way. Maybe I've got a complex or maybe——"

"Sara," interrupted Caroline, who considered she knew Sara's character and saw no particular point in discussing it, "what about going to St. Quay—in the little train, of course: I'm not walking that foul road again—this afternoon? We could bathe maybe for it might not be such a dull day there. Actually, if we were at home we'd think this was a really good day, no rain or wind. It's only that we've been spoiled with all that sun. Think of it!—sun every day for a month."

"'Mm, gorgeous, isn't it? I'm always going to go abroad for my holidays now," said Sara importantly. "And I think St. Quay might be fun. Even if we don't bathe we can go to the *pâtisserie.* . . ."

They had to bolt lunch and dash like lunatics to St. Brioc station to catch the only suitable little train, but they managed it.

"There's a nice easy-going atmosphere about this country that I like," said Sara, as the little train kindly waited at the next station for an old peasant to go back home and fetch a basket of eggs she had forgotten. "Fancy a B.R. train waiting for you to go home and collect eggs!"

"It might be a nuisance, this kind of thing, if you were in a frantic hurry," Caroline said reasonably.

"Nobody ever is, here, I should think," said Sara. "And another thing I really do like, is being able to talk about people, right to their faces nearly, and saying maybe the rudest things, and they don't understand a word. They just smile." Sara's bright little face certainly did meet smiles wherever it went, perhaps because she smiled first, and the entire long carriage in the little train—with its motley assortment of Breton women in white caps, huge baskets on their knees, or men with long pipes, Parisian families on holiday, the children clutching spades and buckets —was no exception, but smiled and exchanged small bits of conversation. Caroline was making hideous faces—her one parlour-trick—to amuse a solemn little boy in knickerbockers and a sailor hat who was by no means sure whether to laugh or howl.

"I mean, look at that fat woman who will keep slapping her young and then kissing them," Sara went on in her clear, carrying voice: "she doesn't know I'm talking about her. And that comic wee pair over there having a scene—what relation are they, do you think? And as for that young man in the corner, what d'you imagine he is? He's very townified and superior, sitting there like an owl and not speaking to any one. With his brief-case and all—is he a lawyer, would you say, come down from Paris to help a horrid rich old miser cut his only son out of his will?"

"I wish I'd never started this," was all Caroline had to say, for the small boy, having decided that the performance was the greatest fun in the world, refused to let her stop and showed unmistakable signs of bursting into tears whenever she tried.

"Kids do go on so," agreed Sara. "*I* don't think you're a bit funny, but he'll choke if he laughs any more. Maybe you'd better stop—although I don't care for him much really, and I'd rather like to see him turn black in the face."

"I daren't," said Caroline desperately, "or he'll yell, and his mamma'll think I'm sticking pins into him or murdering him or something."

"I have a pin, if you'd like to try," Sara offered, missing the point entirely. "I say, Caro," she continued, "I've been watching the people get out at the stations and nobody seems to collect any tickets, there's no barrier or anything. *Isn't* it a blow we were so honest? We might easily have cheated. The old boy in the ticket-office at St. Brioc probably gave us that great sheaf of tickets, which we thought was silly, because he was so glad to get a sale at last. Probably no one has a ticket but mugs like us. We'll know the next time—St. Quay, Caroline, come on."

"Just in time, let me tell you. My face would have stuck if I'd had to go on another moment. Good-bye, you little horror, *good*-bye."

As they wandered away from the station a quiet voice said in English behind them, "You weren't the only mugs—I've got a ticket too," and they spun round to see the Parisian lawyer, suit-case in one hand and brief-case in the other, regarding them unsmilingly. "Although I was disgusted to hear any country-woman of mine planning in cold blood to cheat the railway company."

"Oh, gosh!" moaned Sara. "You didn't hear

me? Oh, help, what did I *say*?" Sara frantically racked her brains to see if she had been particularly awful, and Caroline, though innocent, was blushing a bright pink.

"Paris lawyer indeed, and me a good Scot like yourselves—the brief-case is for the things I forget to pack."

"Oh dear, are you *furious*? I'm terribly sorry, really I am," said Sara earnestly, "but you see I always put my foot in it."

"How did you know we were Scots?" said Caroline.

"Ha, ha! Yes, of course I'm furious, but I want some tea very badly and need you to show me where to get it." Sara and Caroline, who really were upset in case they had been hurtful as well as rude, were mightily relieved and led the way to the *pâtisserie*.

"I'm here to learn the language," their new friend told them, "going to stay with a family, and I suppose I ought to go and find them, but I don't think I could face any more French just at the moment——"

"That's just like us," said Sara, "only our family is simply frightfully decent and friends of Caroline's mother. That's Caroline there, she never speaks: and my name is Sara Storm. Have you got a name?"

"Not I. I am the Man of Mystery. Is this the place? Could you eat something, if you tried very hard?" The girls did try very hard and succeeded in putting away a very fair quantity of cakes, advising the Man as to the best ones. After that they had to abandon all thoughts of bathing lest they should sink like stones. So they lingered over tea and Sara chattered, about adventure and one thing and another, and the Man of Mystery told them he was up at Oxford and was sure he knew a man there who had been at school with Sara's eldest brother; and then they had a walk round, and he finally put them on to their train lest they should try to cheat the railway after all, and they promised they would come back again one afternoon and find him, and his real name, and he must come to Petit Chose——

"Madame will love to have you," Sara said hospitably.

"Well, I'll send you a telegram, and you must arrange a really happy day for me," he told them. Caroline said she hoped he would find his family all right and that they wouldn't be too bad; and the Man of Mystery said that he was sure he would, and that he felt stronger now and ready for anything. . . .

"Oh, Caro," Sara bounced back on her seat after waving good-bye frenziedly, "we do have

fun! D'you think he really is some one mysterious? A famous detective on a secret mission or
something?

"At that age? Not he. He was only playing up
to you and your daft notions when he saw the way
your eyes popped. We'll probably never see him
again."

Sara refused to take this gloomy view, and after
much cogitation finally came to the conclusion
that he was really a prince in disguise trying to
win back his lost throne, and that she, Sara
Storm, would help him to regain it.

CHAPTER XIII

SARA DOES SOME RESCUE-WORK

THE rain came that night in good earnest, and the wind howled round Petit Chose; windows rattled and doors banged, and Sara woke up in the middle of the night to find herself lying in a pool of water. Her efforts to shut the window roused Caroline.

"What are you doing?" she demanded.

"Trying to shut this beastly window," Sara panted.

"Well, don't, or we'll suffocate."

"I'd rather suffocate than drown," Sara told her. "My bed's soaking."

"Oh, all right!" Caroline grumbled. "Here, I'll shut it. The other one can stay open. Hop in beside me. And don't blether, because we're going to be called early, if it's nice, to go to the Mount, and I want to sleep. Although you're such a wriggler I probably won't get a wink."

"How harsh you are to me," said Sara plaintively. "I'll lie as still as anything and you'll never know I'm here."

By some of her extraordinary contortions, Sara's head was at the bottom of the bed when

178

Louise came in next morning, her foot nearly poking Caroline's eye out, but Caroline seemed unmoved, and to have got some sleep, for she was quite bright and, for her, eager to be up and off on their little excursion.

Raymond and Papa had some manly scheme on hand so the females set off alone with Madame at the wheel, a very healthy-looking picnic basket sharing the back seat with Sara.

They bought a yard-long loaf in Kerdic, which Sara tucked into the book-rack on the roof, but which was apt to jolt loose and catch her a vicious blow on the head when she was least expecting it. They stopped for a little at St. Malo, and Madame showed some eagerness to take them to see Châteaubriand's tomb on its little island. She was foiled by the tide being high, much to Sara's glee, for she had never heard of Châteaubriand and had certainly no desire to see his last resting-place. But they enjoyed walking round the ramparts, although Sara would try to peer through the windows of the houses built against them, Caroline very nervous lest the house-holders should issue wrathfully forth at this invasion of their privacy. They were pleased with the Grande Rue, grand in name only, for it was narrow between tall houses, and steep and twisting, and altogether delightful.

Sara was reluctantly dragged away from the shops, but was consoled by the next part of the journey. It even brought a word of praise from Caroline, hitherto very unenthusiastic about the scenery. She liked the bleak, bare coast, and Sara was thrilled with the little thatched houses and frequent old windmills. In one, which had been smartened up, she wanted to jump out and live, there and then, but Caroline vowed it would be over-run with mice and Sara who, to her shame, had a horror of such creatures, agreed to go on more willingly. Before Pontorson, six miles from the Mount, they stopped and had lunch in a field, the loaf proving none the worse for its contacts with Sara's skull.

They did not linger long, but pushed on until Madame said, "Look! The Mount!" and they saw the great rock rising, its base girt round by mediæval walls and towers, crowned with little houses and the Abbey, joined to the mainland by a causeway. Sara was glad she had her glasses on, for it was an exciting sight, and Madame told them how lucky they were to see it at high tide.

They left the car, and passed through the Porte de l'Avancée, the only opening in the ramparts, and Madame rather proudly pointed out to the girls the two cannon which the English had abandoned when they had unsuccessfully besieged the Mont St. Michel in the fifteenth century. Caroline was frankly incredulous that the English had besieged any French stronghold without success, but she had no time to argue, for they went through two other ancient picturesque gateways, and the sight of the one street, a narrow lane with gabled and overhanging houses, climbing up at its farther end by slippery and cobbled steps to the Abbey, was greeted with a chorus of Ohs and Ahs of appreciation.

When, after mounting many stairs, they reached the Abbey, Madame was determined that their minds should be improved and joined a party starting the rounds with a guide. Caroline drank in every word, but poor Sara was frankly bored. She annoyed the guide very much by constantly lagging behind, and the guide annoyed her by waiting each time, before beginning his little lecture, until she appeared—to face the black looks of the assembled crowd of sight-seers.

In the *Crypte des Gros Piliers*, when the guide was declaiming what was surely, thought Sara, pretty obvious to any one, namely that it was so called from its enormous columns, she decided that she could bear it no longer, and faded quietly out of the crowd. No one, least of all the guide, was paying the slightest attention to her at this point, but it pleased her to think that only by great stealth and cunning could she make her escape; so, feeling like an Indian brave or one of her beloved sleuths, she dodged and sidled round the pillars, bent nearly double, and peering frequently round the great stone columns to see if she had been spotted. Caroline, as a matter of fact, noticed her antics at one point and wondered fleetingly what Sara thought she was doing, but she moved on at the guide's heels and forgot her.

Sara, having gained, after a perilous journey, the entrance, raced through the dark passage and the other crypts they had already visited, and upstairs as hard as she could go; she wandered, more circumspectly but still stealthily, through the church to a side-chapel, contemplated investigating a flight of stairs, but again turned tail as she heard the sounds of a rival party descending; decided that what she wanted was fresh air and something to eat, and came out on to the terrace before the church. It was quiet here, no one to be seen, and, abandoning her scouting manœuvres, she straightened up and started down the great flight of stairs quite normally.

It was on the thirtieth step down—Sara was counting them because she was sure Caroline was wrong when she said on the way up there were only ninety, and not at least a thousand—that she discovered the child. And the child was crying.

Quite softly, but quite unmistakably crying, not a soul near her as she sat on the step in her little blue dress, her little fat fists knuckling her eyes.

Sara was touched to the heart, but perfectly ignorant as to any means of tackling the situation. She sat down beside her and said, "Hullo!"

The child took one look at her, and her soft crying changed to a hearty roar.

"Gosh, I don't seem to have said the right thing!" thought Sara, so without further polite skirmishing she plunged straight into things and said, during a small lull:

"What's the matter?"

The child roared louder than ever.

"There, there, don't cry, little cabbage," Sara said, and ran through all the French endearments she could think of, followed by literal translations of English ones, each new effort being greeted by a lustier bellow than the one before. Sara was being reluctantly forced to the conclusion that the infant had taken a dislike to her on sight when she saw a gleam of hope. Scrabbling in her bag she brought out a piece of Toblerone, rather tattered as to its wrappings but still recognizable. The crying stopped as suddenly as if a tap had been turned off. Sara broke a piece and handed it to the child, now turned towards her and solemnly watching her with wet, black eyes.

Having swallowed it the child smiled, a very small watery one, but still a smile. Sara was enormously gratified to see it, and grinned at her.

"*Bonjour*," she said.

"*Bonjour*," said the child.

"Why do you cry?" said Sara.

"I'm lost," said the child.

"Oh!" said Sara, and gave her another bit of chocolate, slipping some back in her bag against future outbursts. "What's your name?" she added. Out of the spate of names which followed Sara managed to distinguish only "Jacqueline," but it seemed to get a good reception when she used it, tentatively. Jacqueline, obviously considering this inquisition to be altogether too one-sided, levelled things up a little by saying:

"What is your name?"

"Sara," said Sara.

"Sara?" the infant tried it. "It is droll, that name." Sara was beginning an impassioned defence of her name when she realised the small critic could not be more than five, so instead she tried to learn more about her. Yes, she had come with Maman and Papa; Maman was walking with a great number of people and Jacqueline did not like it, so she had come for a little promenade by herself. No, Papa was not with Maman. She did not know where Maman was, and her lower lip began to quiver so dangerously that Sara hastily stopped it with another piece of chocolate.

"So that's how it happened," thought Sara. "Maman will think Papa has the poor child, and I suppose Papa thinks that Maman has her. Gosh, people are funny—bad enough trailing round these mouldy old walls by yourself without carting a child with you besides. Oh, well, I suppose we'd better go and look for Maman. Come, Jacqueline," she said aloud with a confidence she did not feel, "we shall find Maman."

But would Jacqueline, who seemed to have grown fond of her hard seat, move? She ignored Sara's outstretched hand and refused to stir. Sara painted as alluring a picture of the finding of Maman as she could, but without avail.

"Well, supposing I carry you?" she said at length, in desperation. Jacqueline smiled a seraphic smile and lifted her arms towards Sara.

"Maman is down there," she said, pointing downwards towards the little street.

"Oh, surely not," said Sara, hitching her burden a little higher. But Jacqueline insisted, so down they went. No sooner had they reached the bottom step than Jacqueline graciously admitted she had made a mistake.

"Maman is up there," she said, pointing upwards.

"I wish you'd make up your mind, little frog," panted Sara. "I should never have listened to you in the first place, only you looked ready to scream the place down. All right, up we go. A little walk, perhaps? No? I thought not."

She was a solid child, was Jacqueline, and Sara, rather scant of breath herself by now, found these ninety steps up difficult going, especially as Jacqueline, besides nearly throttling her rescuer with her arms, seemed to think a little light conversation was called for.

After many a halt, however, they did finally reach the top, to see an obviously infuriated mob—led by a small woman in a red hat, a dark man in a straw hat, and three guides in no hats at all—advancing along the terrace.

At the sight of Sara and her load, the crowd halted, as one. Madame Red Hat pointed an accusing hand.

"There she is, there she is, the wicked abductor," she screamed, and the crowd surged forward menacingly. Sara, taken completely by surprise, made an instinctive movement to turn and flee. Fortunately, the thought of staggering down those awful stairs again restrained her. Or maybe it was the sight of Madame appearing at the edge of the throng, with Caroline's grinning face over her shoulder; and shrinking back from the avenging mother who was rushing forward to snatch her child to safety, she called out in English:

"For the love of goodness, Madame, call off the mob! Tell them I didn't steal her—I found her." So Madame stepped forward and poured oil on these troubled waters, and after a rather fierce altercation managed, with Sara's agitated evidence, to convince Madame Red Hat and her spouse that it would not be just to have Sara thrown over the ramparts, or removed to prison. And Jacqueline, who all this time continued to cling to Sara, giving her face and head friendly little pats, almost knocking off Sara's glasses and seriously impeding her story, helped to bring home to Maman that she had been in good hands and was reluctant to leave them. Finally, however, after being presented with the remainder of the chocolate, she allowed her mother to take her and fuss over her extravagantly. Madame Red Hat then expressed her sorrow at doubting such an obviously charming *jeune fille* and shook Sara by the hand. Monsieur her husband shook Sara by the hand, the three guides shook Sara by the hand, and the crowd smiled its approval. Sara was so dazed that she found Caroline shaking her by the hand without surprise. Madame laughed at them both, and suggested that one of the Mont St. Michel's famous omelettes would be just the thing for all three of them.

"The next time," said Sara decidedly, as they sat in a tiny, dark restaurant, Chez Michel, eating the delicious stuff, "the next time, if I'm spared, which I doubt, we go to look at historic monuments, I'll *look* at historic monuments and not try any noble works of rescue."

CHAPTER XIV

CAPTURE OF A CAR-THIEF

"WHAT'S the date?" mumbled Sara, sitting at the bureau writing letters. She never knew the date, and it was a pernicious habit of hers that although by lifting her eyes to a calendar or her hand to a newspaper she could have discovered it for herself, she invariably asked, "What's the date?" If there was no one to ask she left it out.

"August the fourteenth," said Caroline, who was lounging in the *salon* window clicking her big knitting pins lazily, enormous sun-glasses on the end of her nose.

"August the fourt—don't be silly, Caroline. But it *can't* be: we've only been here about a fortnight, and don't you remember, darling, we got away early from school so that Vanessa could bring us? You're raving."

"We've been here seven weeks to-morrow," said Caroline. Sara left off her writing, which bored her anyway, to stare at her in dismay.

"But Caroline, that means we've only three more weeks! But I can't bear it—I couldn't bear to leave Petit Chose!"

"No. It will be rather grim."

"But Caroline, we simply can't go in three weeks—we haven't had any adventures yet!"

"Oh, I dunno—you were nearly carried away in a French battleship; you nearly saw a ghost; you nearly caught a burglar. It may not have been as exciting as you would like, but it has given us many a laugh."

"But Caroline, something always went wrong with these adventures. I want the *real thing*."

"I expect adventure would be nasty in real life, so I shouldn't hanker for it. Much more important, my infant, is the fact that it's Madame's fête next Friday. And what are we going to give her? I had great hopes once of this beastly bed-jacket, but look at it!" Indeed Caroline's pattern could not have been so foolproof as she had imagined, for it had developed, under her inexpert guidance, into a huge, rather soiled pink woollen blanket, quite shapeless.

"You've forgotten the sleeves," said Sara.

"No, I haven't. The sleeves are there."

"But there are no holes for your arms to go through."

"No, neither there are," said Caroline, rather surprised. "Yet I'm sure I remember casting off like anything at one point—and that was supposed to be for a sleeve. Well, it'll just have to be a shawl. D'you think Madame could make use of a nice shawl?"

"She might. But that's the most revolting thing I ever saw in my life—more like a bloated and overgrown scarf. And what is this fête business, anyway?"

"Well, these funny French people apparently have them. Raymond told me—instead of having a birthday you have a—a saint's day, I think it is. According to your name."

"What I'd like," said Sara, "would be to have a birthday *and* a saint's day. I never did think one birthday a year was enough. Is there a saint called Sara, do you suppose, or do the French have the name of a saint pushed in besides their other names? Yes, I think both—it's the best idea I've heard of for a while: I'll start it whenever I get back, and if I call myself all sorts of saints' names I'll have lots of fêtes——"

"You may have forgotten, in your excitement, but it's Madame's fête we're supposed to be discussing."

"Oh, yes! We must give her the most beautiful and unusual and exciting presents she's ever had. Could I get my cushion-cover done in time, do you think? Now, what's the joke? You are queer, Caroline—laugh at nothing sometimes. Oh, I see. 'Mm, perhaps you're right, although it's jolly fine all the same, my cushion-cover. Anyway, I don't think I could ever get it finished."

"Well, she's terribly keen on chocolates—and I think I'll give her that."

"Nice, of course, but not very exciting. I'd like to give her something she wants terrifically and yet wouldn't buy for herself. St. Brioc's no good; St. Brieuc's a bit better but not much; St. Malo—I know! Dinard's the place—fashionable and all that: there are bound to be marvellous shops there."

"But how do we get to Dinard? Pity we didn't think of it on the way to the Mount and we could have stopped there when we were at it. I don't suppose Madame would let us go by train. She's a bit fussy about our going about alone."

It must have been the direct intervention of Providence which prompted Madame next afternoon when she had read her letters to say:

"Would it amuse you, my children, to accompany me to Dinard next Wednesday? Some of my very good friends are there now and would like us to call."

"Oh, Madame, rather," Sara beamed, making so many grimaces and obvious signs of joy to Caroline that the latter wondered if Sara thought she was absolutely dense, and didn't see how Madame could fail to suspect something.

"Will there be room for us, Madame?" she asked.

"Ah, but yes, Caroline, certainly. Armand does not like to make visits; but you and Raymond and I shall go."

Raymond, however, did not go. On Tuesday afternoon, Caroline came thoughtfully into the *salon*, to find Sara alone, reading a thriller Madame had lent her and eating a peach.

"What's the matter with Madame?" Caroline demanded. Sara looked up rather vacantly.

"I didn't know anything was the matter," she said; "she seemed all right."

"Well, I met her just now going into her room —and she had been crying." Caroline looked acutely distressed and uncomfortable at the memory, so to relieve her feelings a little she turned fiercely on Sara.

"Have you been upsetting her?"

"Me? Upset Madame? Of course not. I think she's just as decent as you do, and you know it. I didn't see anything wrong——"

"You wouldn't."

"We were all in here—at least, Papa was in the garden—when the post came in—there's a letter for you, by the way, and something to pay. I say, Caroline, I know. Raymond got a letter. He said something to Madame, who clapped a hand to her head and said, "Ah! Mon Dieu!" Then they both went out to Papa and I could hear them yattering away. Do you think——?"

"'Mm. Failed in his exam. again. Isn't it rotten? And if they only had some stupid money he could go into the Army where he'd be happy."

"Philippe's treasure——" said Sara.

"Oh, don't be such an idiot! You know we've poked round that ruin till Madame got frantic in case some of it would fall and she'd be left with two corpses on her hands."

Their surmise was right. Raymond came in and told them the sad news himself a little later.

"I think he minds, you know," Caroline told Sara, in bed that night. "He's so—so comic and gay you never know whether he does or not, but he's not making so many jokes about this. Of course, I don't know what else he expected, for he didn't do a stroke of work."

"Expected to be made President——" Sara began, and Caroline said very sharply:

"Oh, shut up!"

"But, Caroline, don't worry: he hates it, but he'll get through next time, and there's nothing we can do. It's rather a blow that Madame won't let him come with us to-morrow, as a punishment. . . ."

By the next day the entire family had recovered

their gaiety, to Caroline's infinite relief, but Madame refused to reconsider her decision.

"No. He is a wicked, irresponsible boy, and I will not have such a one with us in Dinard: besides, he likes Dinard, and he is devoted to the de St. Mauriacs because they are often foolish enough to take him horseback-riding in Paris, so it will be very good for him not to go."

Raymond only grinned his impish grin, and waved them good-bye good-naturedly before bounding off to the *grève* to mess about with his canoe and half-drown himself.

They reached Dinard in time to bathe in the *piscine*. After that, and lunch with the de St. Mauriacs in their hotel, where the two felt like tramps, Madame, knowing how they liked to explore, sent them away on their own, with instructions to meet her at the car park at half-past three, and she would lead them to a truly magnificent *pâtisserie*.

They wandered along the Promenade des Alliés, past big hotels facing the *plage*, while Sara, with dim memories of great doings at Monte Carlo by people in the books she favoured, showed a disposition to linger near one of the Casinos.

"We could go in and win a lot of money at the gaming-tables—break the bank, whatever that may mean—and give it all to Madame," was her kind suggestion.

"I don't suppose they'd let us in," said Caroline, "and we might not win."

"People in books always win," Sara said confidently, "and if they don't they shoot themselves."

"I wouldn't care for that at all," Caroline walked firmly away, Sara trotting by her side, the scheme abandoned without much regret, her knowledge of the procedure being vague in the extreme. "What rotten books you do read."

"I like this place," said Sara. "It's bright and sunny and the cliffs are lovely."

"'Mm, I do too. If this were at home I'd loathe it, but it's different here: and it doesn't seem to matter looking a sight in a French town."

They discovered some delightful shops. Outside a very smart one, which had little but a trail of organdie and a handbag in the window, they stopped to admire a wooden brooch.

"Now, Madame would like that," Caroline said. "Go in and ask how much it is."

"I wouldn't dare. Go yourself."

"You know I hate asking: you go, Sara." So the unfortunate cat's-paw went. She was gone a long time, and Caroline was contemplating a rescue when she shot out.

"Well?" asked Caroline.

"Gosh, this is no place for us. Let's get away. Do you know that mouldy wee brooch was a hundred and fifty francs?"

"So I suppose you bought half a dozen."

"No!" Sara was apt to take Caroline's remarks literally. "I just sneered at it and said I didn't really like it very much, and the girl started hauling out others and I thought I'd never get away and I was terrified."

Caroline was repentant and promised not to send her into another lions' den. They bought a big box of chocolates for Caroline's present, and had a good look round, thoroughly enjoying a little civilisation for a change. They came to rest outside a most exciting sort of shop, its small window full of bottles of scent and bath-salts, and gay powder-boxes which gleamed with all manner of colours.

"Scent, now," said Sara, sniffing the fragrance which came faintly from the doorway: "I love scent."

"You're like Daddy," said Caroline. "He always used to give Vanessa and me a jar of ginger every Christmas."

"But you hate ginger."

"I know. He loves it."

"Oh, but Caro, of course I want to give Madame

something she likes. She couldn't *not* like scent, could she? Although she never wears it."

"Well, she wouldn't anyway, fathead, messing about in the country in old cotton dresses and espadrilles. But as a matter of fact, I think I do remember her saying once she had rather a pash on it—when you were showing her that silly little bottle of eau-de-Cologne Aunt Matilda gave you for travelling."

"Good!" said Sara. "When I'm properly grown up," she went on in a dreamy voice, drifting towards the door, "I'm going to buy gallons of scent, and bathe in it, and drench myself in it, even if I'm only wearing rags."

She chose a fat little bottle of thick, clear crystal, smooth and uncut, through which the scent glowed, green as an emerald; and tiny ones, lest the Customs should clap them in gaol, for their mothers, and a powder-box, very smart, for Vanessa.

"Sara, you lunatic, don't open Madame's bottle—it'll evaporate if you let the air in," Caroline scolded as they made for the car-park, seeing that Sara had unwrapped the bottle and was fumbling with the stopper.

"Not just for one wee smell?" said Sara wistfully.

"Don't be so daft; the woman let you smell

some of the same in the shop. As a matter of fact I thought you were going to stay there all day, sniffing."

Sara put her purchase away then, regretfully, into her bag.

"We're early for Madame," she said, consulting her watch. "We could drop all this stuff and do some more exploring."

They reached the spot where they had left the car in time to see a pair of white-flannelled legs disappear inside it and drive it away.

"Well, of all the cheek!" exploded Sara. "Pinch the car under our very nose, would he? What a *mercy* we came back early. Caroline, we *must* follow him. Oh gosh, we can't, of course. Look, what luck, a taxi!" She pushed Caroline into the taxi which was cruising in their direction just then and, as she had always longed to do, said to the driver between shut teeth, "Follow that car!" quite in the style of her approved authors. The effect was rather spoiled because in her excitement she said it in English, and had to repeat it in French, although, as she confided later to Caroline, it didn't sound nearly so dramatic in French.

"Are you sure it's Madame's car?" Caroline asked nervously, as they followed the green Citroën along the Boulevard Président Wilson and right along the Rue de la Poste; "it's a fairly common model. What's her number?"

"543:F:2—I remembered it because of the sequence." Sara was leaning forward, her very nose quivering with excitement, pointing and giving directions to the driver, who could have managed very well without, but considered it all to be another of those queer games the English liked to play.

"That's 543:F:2 all right. But maybe it was M. de St. Mauriac——"

"Far too tall. It's a crook, I tell you. But we'll foil him yet." The crook seemed to be making things easy for his foilers, for he did not hurry himself and finally drew up before a shop, left the car, and airily disappeared within.

"Got him," said Sara. "We'll find a policeman —you could do that, Caroline"—Caroline looked ready to sink into the ground with horror at such an idea—"while the taxi-man and I see he doesn't get away." The taxi-driver, taken into partnership, was heart and soul with the girls. He pointed out a policeman on the other side of the street and willingly went to fetch him over.

"Sara, suppose we've made a mistake?" said Caroline. Sara wouldn't listen.

"There's no mistake," she said. "this is Adventure. Why, it's even a chemist's shop. He's probably buying some awful drugs, or something to stain his skin for a disguise at this very minute!" and she stopped arguing with Caroline in order to explain the situation to the *gendarme*. As she did so, and the *gendarme* inspected the Citroën and the girls in turn, and the taxi-driver discoursed on his share, passers-by sauntered up, eager to see what was going on, until a respectable little crowd had assembled on the pavement. It parted suddenly to let a tall young man in white flannels walk from the chemist's shop through a lane of staring faces to where Sara, still talking, Caroline, wishing she were a hundred miles away, the *gendarme*, and the taxi-driver formed an isolated little group by the Citroën.

Caroline looked up from her intent study of the toe of her right shoe and clutched Sara's arm.

"Sara!" she gasped. Sara whirled round, saw the young man and collapsed on to the running-board of the car.

"Oh gosh, Caroline! The Man of Mystery! Oh gosh," she wailed, "there must be some mistake—he *can't* be a crook. I couldn't bear it."

The Man of Mystery shook Caroline's limp hand.

"Dr. Livingstone, I presume?" he said, grinning

at her. "What are you two doing here? And why the gallery? And a policeman, too! Have you," he said severely, "been cheating the railway again?"

"It's not us, it's you," answered Caroline. "You pinched our car."

The *gendarme*, who could not make head nor tail of this hob-nobbing between accusers and accused, proceeded to assert his authority.

"Oh, do go away, you silly man," Sara muttered crossly in English. "Tell him to go away, Caroline. We can't give the Man of Mystery in charge."

Caroline, assisted by the accused, apologised to the *gendarme* as well as she could for troubling him and lamely explained that there had been a mistake, and that Monsieur the thief was a very old friend. The representative of law and order unwillingly took himself off, followed by the disappointed crowd who had expected great things of this little affair, the taxi was paid off, and the Man of Mystery sat down on the running-board beside Sara.

"Thank you for not handing me over to the police, Sara," he said gravely. "Now will you tell me what I'm supposed to have done?"

Sara, too heart-broken that her prince in disguise should turn out to be a thief in disguise, refused to speak, so Caroline, rather embarrassed, explained the situation.

"Honestly this car doesn't belong to your Madame, you crazy children," he laughed, when she finished. "It belongs to mine: she let me borrow it to-day. Look inside: my camera, although I could have planted that, of course, Madame des Forêts' rug, maps with ' des Forêts ' written on them——"

Sara, beginning to hope, was shaken by this evidence. "But the number——" she said doubtfully, "in sequence."

"Oh, any one can mistake a number," the Man of Mystery said sweepingly, "especially in sequence. We'll go back and find your car and then you'll believe an innocent man."

So they piled in and returned to the car park, where sure enough they discovered the green Citroën's twin, its number plate bearing the legend 543:P:2.

"I suppose," said Caroline witheringly, "that you never happened to look at our number when you had your glasses on."

"Well, you needn't be so snotty—you didn't even know it," Sara replied, but she was too glad to be able to reinstate the Man of Mystery among her heroes to wrangle with Caroline, and too anxious to make amends for having doubted him.

"The whole thing is," said Caroline, as they sat in 543:P:2 waiting for Madame, "it all comes of your being so mysterious. What *is* your name?"

"John Smith," said the name's owner apologetically.

"Well, of course nobody would believe that," Caroline laughed; "much too like an alias——" But Sara was saying to herself, without the least intention of being cheeky, too:

"John Smith, John Smith, now where have I heard that name before?" Caroline giggled, but Sara suddenly jumped, "*I* remember, in *Le Matin* the other day. I don't suppose," she said wistfully, "you could be *that* John Smith, the undergraduate who's been doing great things in the air, flew to New York and back in half an hour or something?"

John Smith hung his head.

"Alas," he said, "I am unmasked. It's too maddening, really," he added crossly, "even you, tucked away in a remote corner of France, heard about it. Only it certainly wasn't half an hour, Sara."

"Well, it's nothing to be ashamed of, is it?" asked Caroline reasonably. "A bit silly, maybe, especially if you had fallen into the Atlantic——"

"Yes, that's what I thought," interrupted John Smith, airing his grievance, "but you should hear my family! You see, it's like this. I'm frightfully keen on flying, but the stern parent simply won't hear of my going into the Air Force —he wants me to be a diplomat, like himself—a diplomat, I ask you——!"

"You would *look* all right," Sara regarded him critically. "Tall and dark and saturnine."

"No, no, Sara, you've got it mixed," said John Smith: "that's the foreign spy. The diplomat is very fair and suave, with an eyeglass. Anyway, I'd loathe it, and I thought, if I do something to show him I really can fly, he'll relent——"

"We always seem to be trying to help square pegs out of round holes," said Sara reflectively. "First Raymond, then you. Sorry, sorry—go on."

"So I did this particular flight, you see, but it didn't work out at all as I expected. It was a stupid thing to try in the first place, and then when it did come off the papers didn't seem to have any nice murders just then and got hold of it, and reporters simply swarmed all over the parent and he was furious. And I must say I got thoroughly fed up with them myself, madmen asking me idiotic questions, so I cleared off here until it should all blow over. And there you are. I don't know why I didn't tell you my name— except that nobody ever believes one could possibly be called John Smith—but I thought I'd pull Sara's leg a bit."

"Well, I thought you were an exiled prince, but it's much more exciting to find you're a famous airman. Can I come flying with you when we get home? I've never been up," said Sara, her eye on the main chance.

"You seem to have missed the point of my long and tedious life-story—my parent does not like me to fly."

"Oh, but he'll come round," said Sara optimistically. "Good, here's Madame. Now we can eat."

They introduced John Smith to Madame who had heard about him from Sara, and they all went off to test the merits of the *pâtisserie* together, and finally parted with mutual goodwill, and John Smith promising a visit to Petit Chose.

Caroline gave Madame the whole story on the way home, and Madame thought that although it was all a mistake Sara had been very brave to go after a thief. "But you must never, never, never do such a thing again, Sara, or you will do yourself a harm."

"She's much more likely to do some one else a harm!" was Caroline's opinion. "Sara," she continued, "there's an awful smell in this car.

Have you been monkeying about with that you-know-what after all I said?" Sara gave a squeak of distress, and grabbed her bag.

"Oh, Caroline, I only opened it a tiny bit, to revive me, when we were in the car with John Smith, and now it's half empty and my bag's sopping! Oh, Madame, your present!" Sara was very upset, and produced the unlucky scent-bottle and Madame had to be told that story, too.

"Ah, but you are too, too kind, my little one—yes, indeed, I insist that you give me it like that, next week, and I shall like it best of all my presents."

CHAPTER XV

MADAME'S FÊTE

"CAROLINE!" Sara's voice came muffled from the folds of a dress she was trying to struggle into, "I can't get this frock on!"

They were changing for Madame's fête dinner, and for this special occasion it was to be their prettiest dresses they were to wear, not just the summer frocks they usually put on at night in place of their shorts.

"I knew I was getting fat," she complained, emerging on the wrong side and throwing the dress disgustedly on the bed, "but I never thought I wouldn't get into it. And it's a pet of a dress, too." So it was, crisp organdie of palest green with little buttons all down the back. Caroline, ready in white, looked sympathetic.

"You will gorge so," she said. "Here, take off that vest and try again. Sara did, and after some ominous creakings at the seams she managed to get it on.

"Does it look awful?" she asked anxiously. "I can hardly breathe and the buttons will never meet, but I've nothing else."

"It doesn't look *too* bad," Caroline said, surveying her: "you did say it was meant to be skin-tight, didn't you? Organdie stretches, anyway. Hold yourself in and I'll have a go at the buttons."

"Well, but it's not much good if I have to hold my breath all night. And I won't enjoy my dinner, which is sickening."

"You'll manage," Caroline muttered, struggling with the buttons. "There! All right?"

"Just. Gosh, this is agony! Caro, you'll need to do my hair, I daren't lift my arms. Throw that jacket round me. Ow!—you're tugging."

Caroline finally passed her as presentable and they went down to the *salon*, Sara moving very warily, although her dress felt easier now, and greeted Mme. Duval. She told them, as if it would be a treat for the two, that her girls and Pierre would be coming over later to play games.

Madame, looking young and pretty, was enjoying her fête as much as a child. The table looked very gay, all decked with trails of pink rambler roses, and the dinner was sumptuous and seemed to Sara to include all her favourite food. There was even champagne in a bucket of ice for the grown-ups, and Sara teased Monsieur until he promised her a thimbleful to drink his wife's health.

"I've never, never eaten such a gorgeous dinner, and I've never had intoxicating liquor before,"

Sara told herself exultantly, watching Monsieur pour a drop into her glass. It was a good party, and Sara had forgotten her dress, so that when Monsieur gave the toast of his wife, she bounced to her feet, much too robustly, what with all the food she had just consumed. With four little pops, four little buttons flew off, like bullets from a gun.

"Oh gosh," thought Sara, feeling the sudden easing of the tension, "I've burst! What on earth shall I do?"

"What's the matter?" asked Caroline in a whisper, under cover of the Duvals' arrival, when dinner was over and they were again in the *salon*, having watched Sara's extraordinary progress thither, sideways round the walls, like a crab.

"I've burst," said Sara. "Have a look and see what's happened."

"Four buttons gone," Caroline giggled after inspection. "You'll have to go and change. You can't stand up against the wall all evening."

Fate intervened for Sara.

"We are going to play hide-and-seek outside, in the dark," Raymond called.

"And you must change your dresses first," Madame said, "or they will be ruined."

"What luck!" Sara crowed—upstairs, hurrying into her shorts.

"Hide-and-seek in the dark is definitely good," said Caroline. "Remember the fun we used to have in your house when we put out all the lights and played?"

Sara remembered very vividly. She had never, as a matter of fact, been able to decide if she simply adored it or quite frankly hated it. It was terribly exciting, of course, creeping about in the darkness, your heart thumping; but it was agony too, not seeing any one, knowing they were there, somewhere, waiting for them to jump out and race you to the den.

In the trees behind the tennis-court it was as black as the pit, but at least you could hear the rustle of the dead leaves, or the snapping of a twig. Sara became more and more worked up, shivering with pleasant terror as she tried to creep back to the den unseen, to elude Raymond, which was no easy task, for he seemed to have eyes like a cat.

Once, when the game had warmed up, and the Duvals' shrieks were coming oftener and louder, Caroline thought she would be a little more ambitious, and went stealthily off to find a hiding-place safe from Raymond, in the old Château. She stole cautiously round the ancient, feet-thick walls, which still partly stood, and found a spot where she crouched. Round her was nothing but the tiny sounds of night, far away she could hear Monique laughing. Feeling cramped, she stood upright, and, thinking what fun everything was and that she had been too clever for Raymond this time, she leaned heavily against the wall to support herself. Slowly, reluctantly, as if loath to give up its secret at the last, the old stone gave way behind her; pushing hard with her back, scarcely realising what was happening, she almost fell through a narrow opening into blackness even deeper than the surrounding night.

"Lumme!" she thought. "The old house is falling to bits. Or can I—possibly—have found—the *passage*!" Excitement rose in her like a flood. "Oh, if only it is! What *colossal* luck! I wish I had a light," she slithered out her foot and felt an unmistakable step descending. "It's not just a hole in the wall, it must be the passage—won't Sara be thrilled? I must find her and get a light. No, I won't—we don't want those Duvals snooping about, we'll wait till the morning. No one will notice the opening for they're all terrified of old Philippe, like Sara, and never come near." Hugging her marvellous secret she circled back, pretending to have come from quite the opposite direction, right into the clutches of Raymond, in despair of her ever appearing. . . .

Caroline could hardly contain herself till Mme. Duval had removed her family, and she and Sara had been sent to bed, Sara protesting as usual, and they were in their room at last.

"If you had tried to stay downstairs another second, Sara, I'd have slapped you. Didn't you see me making signs?" she said.

"Yes, I thought you had gone nuts," said Sara. "I didn't want to come to bed. Wasn't it a lovely party? I never——"

"Shut up, or I'll explode," Caroline interrupted. Sara looked up from unfastening her shoes, to see her calm Caroline excited and flushed, her eyes shining.

"What's biting you?" she asked. "Your face is bright red. Are you ill?"

Caroline ignored these ridiculous questions.

"I think," she said solemnly, "I'm not sure, but I *think* I've found the secret passage."

CHAPTER XVI

THE LAST ADVENTURE

SARA, nearly out of her mind with excitement, had vowed she wouldn't close an eye all night, but it was Caroline, for once, who roused her next morning.

"Get up, fat one," she said, "it's a quarter to seven, and I think we should have a look at the passage before Louise brings breakfast in case anybody gets there first."

"Gosh, it's a miracle!" said Sara, looking in amazement at her fully dressed cousin. "Do I wash, or not?"

"Yes. No. Do what you like, but hurry. I've got two candles and two boxes of matches. Put on your specs. I don't want you falling and breaking your neck."

"Hope old Philippe isn't about." Sara had a momentary qualm as they undid the *salon* window and crept out past the tennis-court. "And I hope you didn't dream it all," she continued pessimistically as they reached the ruin.

But Caroline had not dreamt it. They found the opening, about five feet high and two feet wide, in the wall of what had apparently been the great hall of the Château, by the side of the remains of a huge fireplace, and partly hidden by bushes.

"I must have leant on the spring, or whatever works it," said Caroline. "Here, light your candle and hold it in front of you in case the air's bad: and mind the steps. They start almost at once, I think. Come on, I'll go first, it's too narrow for us both."

They cautiously began the descent: the steps had crumbled away in places, but they managed with caution, hugging the rough walls, to reach the bottom safely.

"Gosh," said Sara, "twenty steps! We're properly in the bowels of the earth now. It's very narrow and going downhill all the way, right through the cliff, I suppose, to the sea."

Caroline was on in front, paying very little attention to Sara's suppositions, shining her candle to left and right without revealing anything but the narrow, low passage, when suddenly, on the right, a sort of little alcove opened out and her heart gave a great leap, for there on the ground lay a small chest.

Just as suddenly she decided, "Sara must find this: she'd adore to find Philippe's treasure—if there is any, and even if it's empty she must find it." So she hastily backed, taking Sara completely by surprise, bumping into her and nearly setting herself on fire.

"You go first for a bit, Sara," Caroline told her; "and I hope to goodness," she added to herself, "the blind bat doesn't miss it."

Sara did not miss it, as her wild yell testified a second later.

"Caroline! A box! A chest! Oh gosh—suppose there is a treasure after all!" Sara was on her knees beside the chest, her candle standing rather drunkenly on the ground. "Caro, I can't move it —it must be stuffed with gold and pieces of eight. And"—with awe—"I found it."

"Pieces of eight, you lunatic!" said Caroline, feeling rewarded by Sara's delight. "Philippe wasn't a pirate. It's probably empty."

"You're an old wet blanket, and just try and move it and tell me if it *feels* empty."

"We certainly couldn't carry it. Shall we go and fetch Raymond and Papa?"

They went back considerably quicker than they had come, and dashing up to Raymond's door, hammered on it, while Sara poured out their story between thumps, in a confused jumble of French and English. When Raymond, wrapped in a dressing-gown, came forth and finally made out what they were trying to tell him he became as wild as Sara.

"I don't think you should expect too much." Caroline tried to prepare Sara for a probable disappointment as they waited for Raymond in the *salon*.

"Rubbish," said Sara, "it's treasure all right, and it was too heavy to cart away."

"Well, why didn't Hubert get it up after he came back to France?" Caroline wanted to know.

"Don't ask such difficult questions. Why doesn't Raymond come?"

Raymond did, just then, with a torch. "I told Maman and Papa," he said. "They are coming, too."

Sara proudly led the whole party, and was most gratified by Madame's and Monsieur's reactions to the sight of the doorway, the passage, and finally the chest.

"We must carry it up, before we try to open it, I think," said Monsieur; and though Sara chafed at this further delay, Monsieur and Raymond, at the cost of nothing more serious than a barked shin, managed to carry it out of its long resting-place into the house. It was not so very heavy, but awkward to manœuvre up the flight of steps.

It lay on the *salon* floor, an ancient wooden box, strongly clasped with bands of iron, a heavy lock protecting its secrets. Monsieur smashed the lock and stood back.

"Sara must lift the lid, I think," he said, and smiled at the small figure fairly quivering with eagerness, half frightened now the moment had come. The lid was stiff, but she wrenched it open and flung it back, while the others watched, tensely and silently.

Her wail of disappointment might have been heard at St. Brioc.

"Books!" she cried, with the utter loathing with which she might have greeted a box of poisonous snakes.

"Philippe's books," said Monsieur in a reverent voice. "Too heavy to take away, and not deemed worth retrieving afterwards." But Madame and Sara looked at each other miserably, both of them ready to cry.

"Beastly, stupid old books, and I was *sure* it was jewels. Leave the horrid things alone, why don't you?" Sara looked murderously at Caroline, who was turning over a small volume with gentle fingers.

"Stop croaking, you ass, they're beautiful. Look at this manuscript, Monsieur—I can't make out a word."

"Old French, Caroline," said Monsieur, becoming more excited as Sara and Madame grew crosser, and rescuing a tome from the hands of the vandal, Sara, who was preparing to heave it into the garden. He talked quickly to Madame and Raymond, who looked slightly dazed and incredulous.

"But Papa, worth thousands of francs, the old books of Philippe?" said Raymond.

"I do not know, Raymond, they may not be worth so very much. But as you can see, they are beautiful, and I think valuable. We should take them to Paris, immediately. My old friend Sureau of the Bibliothèque Nationale will advise us: the air may be harming them although Philippe has left them well protected."

Caroline was hanging on every word, but Sara was still scowling and muttering to herself, "Unlucky, that's what I am. Anybody else finds a treasure-chest, and it's full of treasure. I—we rather, for it's all Caroline's doing—find a chest and what's in it? Mouldy old books. And not even readable at that. Beautiful! All yellow and musty and the pictures like postage stamps. Gosh! They've gone mad—where are they off to with the blooming chest? If it's a bonfire, I don't want to miss it——"

But the chest was snatched from under her nose and put carefully into the little car, while Monsieur and Raymond, after making themselves presentable for Paris, bundled in after it, and waved Madame and the girls farewell.

"Will somebody," said Sara plaintively, waving vigorously but with little understanding, "*please* tell me what's happening. . . ?"

Although the three in the *salon* were waiting for nothing but a telephone call from Monsieur in Paris, next morning, when it did ring they jumped like shot rabbits, and were all standing stiffly when Louise came in and announced that Mademoiselle Caroline was wanted.

"Me?" said Caroline. "Who was it, Louise?"

"I do not know, Mademoiselle. I could not make out the name."

"Who on earth wants to speak to Caroline?" Sara fretted. "Oh dear, it's almost too much for me, all this excitement." Caroline's voice coming indistinctly from the hall laughing and talking scarcely increased her patience, so that when Caroline came back she said, "Who *was* it, you grinning ape?"

Caroline's grin broadened at this welcome. She said, "It was the Man of Mystery. He's sorry, Madame, he won't be able to come to-morrow——"

"I had forgotten that he was coming," said Madame guiltily.

"——because he's going home. It's lovely, Sara—the stern parent has repented: went up to one of the Hebrides for a holiday, developed acute appendicitis and was only removed to a nursing-

home in time—by aeroplane! So he became all
abject and had son John cabled that all was for-
given, that he could fly till he burst. Or so John
Smith says. Fun, isn't——"

The telephone's clamour interrupted, and this
time all three made a wild dash for the hall.

"'Allo, Armand? Yes, it is I," Madame's voice
was a little high and strained. Caroline was
making some pretence at manners, staring nonchalantly out of the hall window as though the
telephone conversation were the last thing to
which she was paying attention. Sara, all her
hopes restored by the thought of the learned
M. Sureau inspecting her find, was unashamedly
listening to Madame's every word, and obviously
only by superhuman effort restraining herself
from snatching the telephone out of Madame's
hand.

"Ah no, it is not possible! Worth so much
money!" Madame made gasps of astonishment
and turned round to smile and give Sara a little
pleased nod. Sara clapped her hands and ran over
to shake the news and some excitement into
Caroline, while Madame, with difficulty in view
of the noise that was going on, finished her
conversation. She came over to the two by the
window.

"M. Sureau says they are a wonderful collection

of books and manuscripts, and if sold would, he thinks, he *thinks*, Sara, raise perhaps a hundred thousand francs!"

"A hundred thousand francs, Madame? Gosh, Caroline! How much is that?"

"Nearly ten thousand pounds." Caroline's wide grin testified to her delight. "But there may be a catch somewhere," she added cautiously. "Maybe no one will want to buy them."

"Well, no one in their senses would, if you ask me," said Sara; "but even half of that! And Madame, Raymond needn't go on with his horrid exam. any more, need he?"

Madame gave Caroline's arm a little pat, and smiled at Sara's eager face with suspiciously bright eyes. "No, Raymond need not go on with his horrid exam any more," she said. . . .

And now it was September the fifth: to-morrow Vanessa and John would arrive in Major Morris, but to-night that dreadful event was not to be thought of, and all was gaiety. The de St. Briocs, Caroline and Sara (mercifully in a green linen dress with plenty of room for expansion) had tucked into another banquet, and now Monsieur was on his feet, making the most beautiful speech which was sending Caroline pink round the ears and convincing Sara that in one second she would howl like a dog, and handing each of them a tiny parcel. Sara thought that if her fingers didn't stop shaking she would never get the tissue paper off; but of course she did, and snapped open the jeweller's box, and not a word came from either Caroline or Sara. For there on their little beds of white velvet sparkled two bracelets, most exquisitely wrought gold links, and on each link hung a tiny book, all shapes, like Philippe's books, some gold, some enamel with dim lovely colours, and on Sara's hung too, a little treasure chest, made of emeralds, while Caroline's had its twin in sapphires.

The long silence was getting on poor Monsieur's nerves.

"Perhaps," he said anxiously, and a little sadly, for he had tried so hard, he and the famous jeweller, to evolve something that would please them, something to remind them absolutely of that exciting day, "perhaps you do not like them?"

Caroline looked up dumbly, her radiant face telling its own tale.

"*Like* them?" choked Sara. "Oh, Monsieur— and Madame—and Raymond," and going all French, she flung her arms round Monsieur's neck and then kissed them all in turn.

THE END

PRINTED IN GREAT BRITAIN